We met in Italy one summer day...

The menu at the bistro had overwhelmed me. Too much to choose from, and the plate of linguini covered with herb sauce wasn't what I thought I'd asked for.

"No, *grazie*," I told the waiter, searching my little phrase book.

"*Per favore, signorina,* may I help?"

I looked up and there he was: tall, dark, handsome and able to speak English. "Yes, please!" I replied fervently. "All I want is a light meal, but not a salad. Just something small."

"I understand perfectly." He engaged the waiter in discussion, and with nothing better to do, I simply stared at my gallant rescuer. He was perhaps five feet ten or eleven, with a slim but powerful build, thick black hair that gleamed under the sun and a face that left me dry-mouthed and reaching for my glass of *acqua minerale....*

"And the next thing, he asked if he could join you," my granddaughter said dryly.

"Actually, I asked him."

"So how long before you decided you were in love with him?"

"About five minutes."

"Oh, come on, Gran! You don't mean that."

"I do. It really was love at first sight, for both of us. Fate's way of letting us know we were meant to be."

Dear Reader,

When I was expecting my second child, my three-year-old daughter wanted to know if I'd still love her as much after the new baby was born. When I assured her I would, she asked, "But what if you don't have enough?"

The Man from Tuscany is Anna and Marco's story, and is about always having enough. The human heart has an infinite capacity for love in all its guises. It is not always convenient, often not easy and sometimes demands a terrible price from those who embrace it. But it binds us as wives, mothers, daughters, friends and lovers. It makes us fallible and gives us our humanity. As Anna says, "We don't choose who or when to love, it chooses us."

May it choose you.

With love,

Catherine Spencer

THE MAN
FROM TUSCANY
Catherine Spencer

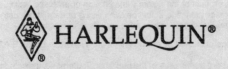

TORONTO • NEW YORK • LONDON
AMSTERDAM • PARIS • SYDNEY • HAMBURG
STOCKHOLM • ATHENS • TOKYO • MILAN • MADRID
PRAGUE • WARSAW • BUDAPEST • AUCKLAND

ISBN-13: 978-0-373-71523-7
ISBN-10:   0-373-71523-4

THE MAN FROM TUSCANY

www.eHarlequin.com

Printed in U.S.A.

ABOUT THE AUTHOR

Catherine Spencer is a former high school English teacher, and a multi-published author with Harlequin, mostly under the Presents imprint. Her books have been distributed in more than thirty-five countries and translated into over twenty languages. *The Man from Tuscany* is her first Harlequin Superromance book. She lives on Canada's west coast with her husband and two adorable yellow Labrador retrievers. She has four children and eight grandchildren—an amazing achievement for a woman who's still only thirty-nine! She loves to hear from her readers and may be contacted through her Web site at www.catherinespencer.com.

Books by Catherine Spencer

HARLEQUIN PRESENTS

HARLEQUIN PRESENTS EXTRA

Don't miss any of our special offers. Write to us at the following address for information on our newest releases.

Harlequin Reader Service
U.S.: 3010 Walden Ave., P.O. Box 1325, Buffalo, NY 14269
Canadian: P.O. Box 609, Fort Erie, Ont. L2A 5X3

CHAPTER ONE

SOMETHING was definitely amiss. Anna Wexley was a creature of habit, and asking Carly to drop everything and visit her on a weekday morning was a marked departure from the usual. A critical care nurse, Carly knew how precariously balanced her grandmother's health was, and how little it would take to tip the scales against her. For that reason alone, she wasted no time driving out to Allendale House, the elegant old mansion that was now a retirement residence, where Anna had lived for the past several years.

At first glance, nothing appeared out of the ordinary. No ambulance waited in the paved forecourt, and the French doors to her grandmother's suite, directly above the building's main entrance, stood ajar. A good sign, surely, on this warm June morning, because Anna loved sitting on her balcony, listening to the birds and enjoying the distant view of Block Island Sound.

Better yet, no sympathetic voices greeted Carly when she signed in at the front desk. Nor, when her grandmother answered her door, was there any overt hint of trouble. Anna had obviously visited the residence beauty salon earlier, and wore the pretty pleated skirt and white blouse Carly had given her the previous Christmas. With pearl studs in her ears and, as always, her gold filigree heart pendant, she looked remarkably well put-together for an eighty-three-year-old with a history of congestive heart failure. On closer examination, though, Carly saw that although her face lit up with pleasure at the sight of her granddaughter, Anna's eyes glowed with a feverish agitation that was anything but normal.

Folding her in a careful hug, Carly said, "You seemed upset on the phone, Gran. Has something happened?"

"I suppose it has," Anna replied tremulously. "Come sit on the balcony and have a glass of lemonade, while I try to explain."

Following her outside, Carly urged her onto the wicker love seat, sat down next to her and pressed two fingers to her grandmother's inner wrist. "What's wrong? Are you in pain? Any difficulty breathing?"

"Not at all, darling girl. I've decided to go to Italy, that's all, and I want you to make the travel arrangements."

"Italy?" Subduing the impulse to blurt out *At your age and in your state of health?* Carly asked instead, "Why Italy, Gran?"

"There's someone there I very much want to see."

Instincts on high alert again, Carly inspected her critically. "Are you talking about a doctor?"

"No, no. Nothing like that." Her grandmother indicated a leather-bound scrapbook lying open on the wicker coffee table in front of her. "I want to visit *him.*"

Carly scooped the book onto her lap, frowning at the grainy photograph of a man in his twenties. "Who's he?"

Anna sighed and traced her forefinger over his features. "It would be easy for me to lie and say he's just an old family friend, but I can't bring myself to belittle what we've always meant to each other, so I'll tell you the truth. He's the great love of my life, Carly."

This time, Carly couldn't hide her shock. "But he can't be. He's not Grandpa!"

"No, precious, he's not."

Although she seemed in complete command of her faculties, Carly wondered if her grandmother was losing it. Had the distant and more recent past merged into one gauzy memory in which neither people nor time were clearly defined anymore? "This is an old photograph, Gran," she pointed out gently. "Do you remember when it was taken?"

"Of course I do. Right before the outbreak of World War Two."

"Ah! So what you're really saying is, this man was your first love, but Grandpa was your *real* love."

"Your grandfather was my husband and I was devoted to him, but not even he could take Marco's place in my heart."

"That name rings a bell. Didn't he visit you once in England, when Mom was little?"

"Yes. He came all the way from Italy to be with me at a time when I desperately needed him."

"Italy?"

"Well, yes, dear," her grandmother said. "Why else do you think I want to go there? Marco lives in Tuscany."

"Oh, Tuscany!" Carly shrugged disparagingly. "It's such a cliché. Everyone goes there."

"Not when I first met him. It hadn't been discovered then. And we were never a cliché."

"What were you, then?" She knew she sounded as

defiant as a child who'd just learned Santa Claus wasn't real, but she couldn't help herself.

"We were…magnificent."

"Did you *sleep* with him?" Carly chose the word deliberately, intending it as a belittlement of what her grandmother and this man had shared.

Anna shot her a reproving look. "Yes, I did. And made glorious love with him, too."

"I thought that sort of behavior was frowned on back then. That girls from good families like yours saved themselves for their husbands. If he was so wonderful, why didn't *he* marry you?"

"He would have, if—"

"If he'd loved you as much as you loved him?"

"Oh, he loved me, Carly. He adored me."

Hating how she felt inside—betrayed somehow, and almost angry with her grandmother for shattering her illusions of one big, happy family—Carly spread her hands helplessly. "Was he already married, then? Was that the problem?"

"No. *I* was the problem." Anna's voice broke. "I didn't have enough faith in us, and by the time I learned my mistake, it was too late."

"Oh, Gran! Is he dead? Is it his grave you want to visit?"

Her grandmother shook her head, making her thinning white hair float delicately over her scalp. "No. Not that death changes the things that matter…the eternal things. One day, I'll be with him forever, and with your grandfather, too. But before that, I want to hold his hand and look in his eyes once more, and tell him again how much I've always loved him."

Carly watched her in silence, then glanced away. "I've

always sensed there was some deep, dark secret that no one in the family ever talked about," she said hollowly, "but not in a million years would I have guessed it was something like this."

"Are you disappointed in me, Carly?"

She shrugged. "In some ways, I guess I am. You and Grandpa always seemed so solid. Mostly, though, I'm confused. Once or twice I've thought I was in love, but it didn't last. But you and this Marco—how many years has it been, Gran?"

"Going on sixty-five."

"How could you bear to be apart from him?"

"Sometimes I didn't think I could. But then I'd think of what I'd have to give up in order to be with him—my dear Brian, my daughter and you, my beautiful granddaughter. And I couldn't bear that, either, because I loved you. You bring me such joy, Carly, and I am so proud to be your grandmother. From the day you were born, we've had a special connection, one I treasure beyond price."

"If he loved you as much as you say, he must have resented me for that."

"No. Marco understood that, for as long as they needed me, my family had to come first."

"And he went on loving you anyway?"

"Yes. Neither of us ever had a moment's doubt about the other."

"How do you recognize love when it comes along, Gran?"

"When it consumes you," Anna said.

Intrigued despite herself, Carly took her hand. "Tell me about him, Gran. Make me understand."

A breeze drifted over the balcony, scented with thyme

and oregano from the herb garden. Anna closed her eyes and smiled dreamily. "I met him the summer I turned eighteen...."

"I WISH I WAS COMING with you," my mother said, layering tissue paper over the clothes in my travel trunk before closing the lid. "But you and Genevieve are such good friends that you won't miss me too much, and with my sister chaperoning, I know you'll be in safe hands."

It was July 6, 1939. My cousin, my aunt and I would take the train to New York the next day, and on the eighth, set sail aboard the *Queen Mary* for Southampton. Originally my mother had planned to make the trip, as well, but ten days earlier, my father had undergone an emergency appendectomy. So she'd decided to stay home to supervise his recovery.

At first, I'd wanted to beg off traveling, too. Seeing my strong, active father confined to a wheelchair and looking so wan had frightened me. But neither he nor my mother would hear of it.

"Of course you must go," they said. "It's expected of girls like you."

My father, you see, was Hugh Edward Leyden, a respected lawyer; my mother, the former Isabelle Jacqueline Fontaine, a member of the Daughters of the American Revolution, active on the board of directors of the Rhode Island Junior League and a prominent Newport society hostess.

As I was their only child, they had great hopes for me to marry well and make them proud. In the 1930s, not a great deal else was required of privileged daughters. If they'd attended the right schools, knew which fork to use, were mannerly, had traveled abroad, could speak a little French or Italian and gave of their time to worthy causes, they were considered a credit to their families.

So there I was, poised to leave on a limited version of the grand tour. Normally we'd have visited several countries, among them Germany and Spain, but Europe was in turmoil and it was decided we were safer to confine ourselves to Italy. We were to "do" Florence, Venice, Milan and Rome, and finish with a few days in Paris if the political climate allowed. At the end of August, I would return home, my enduring passion for great art at least partially satisfied, my exposure to the rich and varied culture of Italy an added bonus to my already sterling pedigree.

The morning we left, our good friends and next-door neighbors, John and Elaine Wexley and their son, Brian, joined my parents on the front terrace to wave us on our way. Brian was twenty-four and home from college for the summer, but despite the six-year age difference between us, we'd been as close as brother and sister since childhood.

"I'm going to miss you," he said, giving me a hug. "Have a wonderful trip, Anna, and stay safe."

Saying goodbye to my family was a tearful business. My mother and I wept unashamedly. My father composed his features into such stern lines that I knew he, too, was struggling to keep his emotions in check.

"Ye gods, Anna!" Genevieve exclaimed, at last managing to pry me away from them and stuff me in the car that was to take us to the railroad station. "Anyone would think you were never coming home again. I hope you're not going to weep your way across the Atlantic. I'm told life on board the *Queen Mary* is one long, glamorous party and I shall take great exception if you're being dreary the whole time."

I smile in reminiscence....

"And were you?" Carly asked. "Dreary, I mean?"

HER GRANDMOTHER laughed. "Oh, no! The minute we boarded the ship, excitement replaced homesickness. We'd heard about the kind of comfort the Cunard Line offered its first-class passengers, but nothing could have prepared us for the luxury. It was said that no two staterooms were alike, and I well believe it. Ours was fitted with inlaid wood paneling and the most wonderful art-deco furnishings. Next door, Aunt Patricia was surrounded by such a wealth of elegance that she hardly ever ventured from her quarters except for meals—which fell in perfectly with Genevieve's plans."

"Genevieve must've been fun. I wish I'd known her."

"My cousin was a hellion!" Anna said with fond nostalgia. "You won't remember her, Carly. She died twenty-one years and three husbands ago, when you were only three, but even all these years later, I smile when I think of her on that ship. Half the crew and most of the male passengers were in love with her before we sailed out of New York. Before we reached Southampton, she'd turned down five marriage proposals and broken more hearts than all the other women onboard put together."

"And what about you, Gran? How many proposals did you receive?"

Anna laughed again. "Oh, Carly, no one noticed me! I was merely the quiet cousin, pleasant enough in my way, but not nearly as vivacious or memorable as Genevieve."

"How unfair!"

"Not at all. I didn't lack for escorts by day or for dance partners in the evening. I just didn't inspire grand passion, that's all—at least, not until we arrived in Florence and I met Marco."

"What made him different?" Carly wondered aloud. "Was it that he noticed you and not her?"

"For a start, she wasn't with me that day. I spent the morning roaming the halls of the Pitti Palace, but she had no interest in art galleries and wanted to go shopping. By then, Aunt Patricia realized that, left to her own devices, Genevieve was likely to run off with the first handsome Italian who caught her eye. I, on the other hand, was *comme il faut,* and could be relied upon to behave appropriately without being chaperoned every minute of the day. So, as much to preserve her own sanity as to protect her daughter's reputation, wherever Genevieve went, Aunt Patricia went, too."

The irony of the situation did not escape Carly, and she couldn't resist a grin. "Leaving you, the good girl, free to have an illicit affair right under your aunt's nose. Did she never suspect what you were up to?"

"Never. As far as she knew, I spent my days absorbing the history of the city and improving my Italian. I was always back at the hotel in time to change for dinner and always spent the evening with her and Genevieve."

"And the nights?"

"Well…" A delicate flush tinted her grandmother's cheeks.

Amused despite herself, Carly said, "Don't tell me you snuck out every night as soon as poor old Aunt Patricia hit the sack, and Genevieve covered for you?"

"Not *quite* every night."

But often enough for an unprincipled rat to put the moves on her naive and trusting grandmother! "So how did you meet this Marco? Was he trolling the halls of the Pitti Palace, looking for innocent young American girls to seduce?"

"He was doing nothing of the sort," Anna said sharply. "I met him over lunch at an outdoor trattoria. He was at the table next to mine. I had trouble explaining to the waiter what I wanted to order, Marco overheard and stepped in to translate...."

THE MENU overwhelmed me. Too much to choose from, and the plate of linguine covered with herb sauce the waiter set before me wasn't what I thought I'd asked for. I hadn't acquired a taste for pasta at that point. We never ate it at home. *"No, grazie,"* I told him, searching my little phrase book. *"Voglio qualcosa...luce."*

"Luce?" He eyed me doubtfully.

"L...i...g...h...t," I enunciated, slowly and very distinctly, the way English-speaking tourists tend to do when abroad and confronted by a foreign language. "I...want...something...light."

"Ah, si! Capisco!" He reached into his vest pocket and produced a small box of matches. *"Sigarette."*

"No!" I exclaimed, shocked by the very idea. *"Non sigarette. No fumo*—I don't smoke."

The waiter threw up his hands, completely at a loss.

To my right, a chair scraped over the piazza's ornately patterned paving stones, and another voice, deep and confident, joined the conversation. *"Per favore, signorina,* may I help?"

I looked up and there he was—tall, dark, handsome and able to speak English. "Yes, please!" I replied fervently. "All I want is a light meal. But not a salad," I was quick to add. I'd been warned to avoid any uncooked foods that had been washed in local water. "Just something…small." I gestured at the linguine. "It's too hot for a heavy meal like this."

"I understand perfectly." He engaged the waiter in discussion, and with nothing better to do, I simply stared at my gallant rescuer. He was perhaps five feet ten or eleven, with a slim, but powerful build, thick black hair that gleamed under the sun, and a face that left me dry-mouthed and reaching for my glass of *acqua minerale*….

"AND THE NEXT MOMENT, he asked if he could join you," Carly observed dryly.

"Actually I asked him. It seemed the mannerly thing to do, considering how helpful he'd been. My Italian was obviously minimal, but his English was excellent. We struck up a conversation and when he discovered my interest in the historical buildings and churches of Florence, he offered to introduce me to his city."

Carly rolled her eyes. "How original!"

"I thought he was very kind—not to mention knowledgeable. He was an architect, you see, and well qualified to give me a guided tour."

"Right! And show you his etchings while he was at it."

"Carly!"

"Well, you can't blame me for wondering! So how long before you decided you were in love with him?"

"About five minutes."

"Oh, come on, Gran! You don't mean that."

"I do. It really was love at first sight, for both of us. *Parafulmine,* Marco called it. A lightning bolt without the thunder. Fate's way of letting us know we were meant to be."

Unprincipled and smooth-talking, as well. Carly couldn't repress the cynical thought. "Did he try to kiss you that first day?"

"He did better than that," her grandmother said, fondling her gold heart pendant. "He proposed."

"He did not!"

"He did. 'Will you marry me, Anna?' he said. And I said I would."

Carly glanced again at the photograph. "Well, he was definitely attractive. I can see how you might've fallen for his good looks."

"Oh, he was so much more than just a handsome face. He was beautiful on the inside, and he brought out the very best in me. That's why I need to see him again, Carly. I need to tell him that, despite all the things that went wrong and all the tears we've both shed, I have never for a moment regretted loving him."

"So it wasn't all moonlight and roses, then?"

Her grandmother gazed off into the distance, seeming pursued by memories. "No," she said slowly. "Sometimes it was pure hell, and I don't know how we survived. But nothing could put a dent in my certainty that he was my other half and we would have our happy-ever-after ending."

"So what happened?"

"The war," Anna said. "Let's go for a breath of fresh air in the garden, precious, and I'll tell you all about it."

CHAPTER TWO

THEY WERE HALFWAY to the gazebo near the pond, sufficiently far from the house that no one could overhear their conversation, but close enough that the walk didn't overtax her grandmother's strength, when Carly noticed a couple heading toward them.

"You've got more company, Gran," she said. "Mom and Dad are here. Did you ask them to stop by?"

Dismayed, Anna said, "Gracious, no! This isn't a story Grace would understand, nor would she appreciate my sharing it with you."

And she wouldn't appreciate finding them together now, Carly thought, aware that her mother had always resented her closeness with Anna.

"Why are you here, Carly?" Grace demanded the second she arrived within hailing distance. "You don't usually stop by during the week."

"It was kind of spur-of-the-moment, Mom. Gran had a little business she wanted me to take care of, and she's in a bit of a hurry."

"What sort of business, Mother? If it's your heart, you shouldn't be wandering around so far from the house."

"It's not my heart, dear," Anna said placidly.

Grace flicked a glance from her mother to Carly, and when neither offered any further explanation, motioned impatiently with her hand. "Then what? Are we allowed to hear or is it a big dark secret between the two of you?"

Carly's father dropped a kiss on Anna's head and urged her to a nearby garden bench. "It's a big dark secret," he teased, attempting to lighten the moment. "Some silver-haired admirer living on the third floor has swept you off your feet, and you're getting married again. Admit it, Anna. You want Carly to help you elope."

Oh, Dad! Carly stifled a horrified giggle. *You have no idea how close to the truth you've come!*

Unruffled, her grandmother said, "Not quite, Taylor. I want to go to Florence, that's all, and I've asked Carly to make the travel arrangements."

"Florence, as in Italy?" Grace fairly choked on the question.

"The very same, dear. It's always been one of my favorite cities."

If she'd hoped to fool anyone into believing she hadn't dropped news on par with a minor earthquake, Grace soon disabused her of that notion. "And Carly, of course, has explained it's absolutely out of the question."

"That was my first reaction," Carly admitted, "but now that I've had chance a to think about it, it doesn't strike me as such a bad idea, after all."

Her mother stared at her, slack-jawed. "Why in the world would you encourage such a foolish request?"

"Why is it foolish, Mom? What's to stop Gran from going to Italy if she wants to?"

"Well, her age, for one thing. And if that's not enough,

how about the fact that she can barely make it from her suite to the dining room without a blast of oxygen to get her there? A journey like this will *kill* her."

"Rubbish, Grace!" Anna declared. "I'm a lot tougher than you give me credit for. Provided I take my medication and travel first-class, both of which I intend to do, I'll be just fine."

"I swear you get dottier by the day!" Frustrated, Grace appealed to her husband. "Taylor, talk some sense into your mother-in-law."

"It is a fair distance for a woman your age to travel alone, Anna, especially considering your health problems," he pointed out mildly.

"I'll hardly be alone, dear. I'm sure Carly will take me to Boston, check me in at Logan, and see to it that I have a wheelchair. And the flight attendants are very kind. They'll keep an eye on me."

But she wasn't winning them over, Carly saw. Her mother's face registered growing outrage. Her father, ever the voice of calm reason when the unexpected or unusual occurred, looked distinctly perturbed. And in truth, Carly herself was beginning to have doubts. Her grandmother's secret might have struck a romantic chord in the telling, but when put to the test, grand passion wasn't stacking up so well against the practicalities.

Her father cleared his throat. "Look, we came by because it's such a lovely day we decided to take you for lunch at that place on the beach you like. Why don't we do that and talk about this some more?"

"That's very considerate of you, Taylor," Anna replied, "but there's nothing to talk about. I've made up my mind, and that's that."

"Why are you being so difficult?" Grace snapped. "Can't you see we're worried about you?"

"I know that, and if joining you for lunch will make you happy…"

"I'm not happy, Mother, but when did that ever keep you from doing what you wanted? And the subject is far from closed. Now, you're going to need a sweater—it's always breezy down by the water. We'll have to hurry, or we'll end up waiting for a table."

Annoyed, Carly said in an aside, "You know she can't keep up with you, Mom. If you're worried about having to stand in line, you and Dad go ahead, and I'll bring Gran in my car when she's ready."

Anna waited until they were alone again, then smiled gratefully at Carly. "Convincing your mother I don't have one foot in the grave tends to sap my energy," she said. "Thank you for buying me a reprieve, precious."

"I figured we need it. We have to decide how we're going to handle this, Gran. If Mom gets an inkling of what's really going on here—"

Anna nodded. "I've stirred up quite the hornet's nest as it is."

"Exactly. Let's not make matters any worse." Carly sent her a glance. "Does she have any idea that you've been in love for years with a man who wasn't your husband?"

"Good heavens, no! Marco and I maintained the utmost discretion. I doubt she even remembers who he is."

But that wasn't necessarily accurate, as Carly discovered when they reached the restaurant and Anna stopped to chat with a friend at another table, leaving Carly a few minutes alone with her parents.

"I checked with our travel agent," her father began as soon as she joined them. "It's just as we thought. There are no direct flights from Boston to Florence. At the very least, your grandmother would have to fly to Washington, then change planes again in Munich or Milan, and I'm afraid your mom might be right, Carly. That's more than Anna can handle. Is there any chance you can talk her into settling for somewhere closer, like Bermuda or the Bahamas?"

"I doubt it, Dad. She's pretty set on Italy."

"I'll bet she is," Grace said with some bitterness. "She probably hopes that if she returns to the scene of her youth, it'll give her a new lease on life."

Taylor nodded thoughtfully. "Nostalgia can be a powerful thing for someone your mother's age, honey."

"Some memories are better left untouched, Taylor. If she goes ahead with this, we'll never see her again."

"I don't agree. Despite everything she's gone through, Anna's never once cracked under pressure. And realistically, if she's determined to take this trip, you can't very well forbid her to go. The best we can do is insist one of us goes with her."

Appalled at what that might lead to, Carly said, "She'll never agree to that."

"She might, if you were to volunteer," her father said reasonably. "After all, you're her beloved only grandchild. You're a nurse, so you're qualified to monitor her health. You recently resigned your hospital position, which means you have the summer free before going back to university in the fall. And as far as I know, you're unattached." He held up five fingers. "Have I missed anything?"

"Yes, Dad," she said, seeing her grandmother coming toward them, and fully aware that where this proposed trip was concerned, three would definitely be a crowd. "Gran might not want me along for the ride."

"Now *that* is something *I'll* talk her into. In fact, I'll insist on it," Grace announced. She barely waited until her mother was seated before wading in. "This whole idea of traipsing halfway around the world all by yourself simply isn't feasible, Mother. Travel is confusing at the best of times, especially for someone your age."

"Well, I'm not dead yet, dear," Anna replied. "I'm able to ask for help, if I need it."

"What Grace is saying," Taylor explained, "is that she— we—would feel a lot more comfortable if you didn't go alone. So we're wondering how you'd feel about Carly joining you."

"Carly?" Her face lit up with pleasure. "I'd be delighted to have her as my traveling companion, provided she doesn't mind being saddled with me."

"I don't mind, if *you* don't," Carly said, sliding her a conspiratorial glance. "I've never been to Italy."

"That settles it, then." Taylor lifted his water glass in a toast. "Here's to a safe, successful trip!"

They all seconded that, Carly's mother with markedly less enthusiasm than the rest of them.

"Cheer up, dear," Anna urged. "Think of it as an adventure, one last glorious fling before I reconcile myself to terminal old age and day trips to Newport."

She would've been wiser to keep quiet, because Grace rounded on her fretfully. "Day trips I can understand. But Italy, Mother? And why *now,* for heaven's sake?"

Carly the nurse understood why, whether or not Carly the granddaughter wanted to acknowledge it. Her grandmother rightly sensed her time was running out but realized that to say so would've been as cruel as revealing the part Marco had played in her life.

"Because I'd like to go to Florence and see the Duomo and Michelangelo's *David* one more time. And because I'd love to be the one to introduce them to my granddaughter," she said instead.

"But where will you stay?" Grace asked. "You've never liked big hotels, Mother."

"With the son of an old friend who lives not far from the city. He has plenty of room and I have a standing invitation to visit anytime. Carly, I know, will be welcome, too."

Defeated, Grace sighed. "And when is this visit to take place?"

"As soon as possible, dear," Anna said.

CARLY SECURED reservations for the following Tuesday, flying via Boston to Washington, and from there to England, where they'd spend the night before embarking on the last leg of the journey to Florence. In the five days before their departure, she took care of all the details, and worried that her grandmother had taken on more than she'd bargained for.

"Even with a night in London, you're going to find the journey tiring," she warned, as they boarded the Boeing 777 for the transatlantic flight. "This part alone lasts nearly seven and a half hours."

But nothing could diminish Anna's enthusiasm. Adding a thick folder to the items to be included in her carry-on bag, she said blithely, "The good news is, I can spend it telling you the rest of my story."

Which would have been fine, Carly reflected morosely— except she was no longer sure she wanted to hear it.

CHAPTER THREE

FINALLY, we're on our way. The seat belt sign is off, the aircraft is headed east, and it's time for me to pick up my story from where I left it last week. I only have until tomorrow to convince Carly that I'm not some foolish old woman pinning all her hopes on yesterday, and Marco wasn't a home-wrecker who came between me and her beloved grandpa.

"I phoned Marco again on Sunday, to tell him you're coming with me," I begin. "He's a little concerned that you might not understand the part he's played in my life."

"I'm not sure I do, Gran," she says.

"I know, darling." I pat her hand. "But you will by the time we get to Florence."

"And how does he feel about having me underfoot all summer?"

"He can't wait for us to arrive." In fact, his last words before we hung up were, *Please hurry. I don't want to be apart from you a day longer than necessary.*

"I wonder if he remembers saying almost the exact same words to me, the first time we said goodbye," I murmur. "Probably not. Men don't usually recall such things, and so much has happened since then. But I remember the moment so vividly that I'm breaking out in goose bumps."

"Well, you don't have to talk about it if you don't want to, Gran," Carly says.

"But I do," I tell her. "How else can I make you understand?"

She shrugs, and I know she won't easily forgive what she sees as a betrayal of her family. Steeling myself, I begin....

ON MY LAST NIGHT in Florence, he was waiting for me at our usual place, near the main door to Santa Maria Novella. A high summer moon glimmered over the black-and-white marble facade of the old church, and laid patterns of light on the deserted flagstones of the piazza.

Hearing my footsteps, he stepped out of the shadows and without a word took me in his arms. I sank against him, imprinting in my mind the solid feel of his body, the scent of his skin, the taste of his mouth on mine, because they were all I'd have to sustain me during the months we'd be apart.

In the morning, my aunt, cousin and I would board the train for Paris, on the first part of the long trip to Southampton, where the *Queen Mary* was scheduled to cross the Atlantic on August 30. "And not a moment too soon," my aunt had fussed as she supervised the packing of our travel trunks. "The sooner we're away from this benighted continent and all its troubles, the better."

"How do I let you go, *amore mio?*" Marco murmured, burying his face in my hair.

The tears I'd sworn I wouldn't let fall clogged my voice. "It's only for a little while." *For as long as it takes me to overcome my parents' objections,* I added silently, knowing they'd resist any idea of my marrying a foreigner, let alone one I'd known so briefly, but resolved that nothing would dissuade me from returning to Florence before year's end. "I'll write to you every day."

"And I to you," he promised. "Not an hour will pass that I won't be thinking of you and preparing for our life together."

After that, we wasted no more time talking. Clasping hands, we hurried along the darkened streets to our special place, the room he'd taken above a bookshop not far from the Ponte Vecchio. Although I'd done my best to brighten it with fresh flowers and candles, I suppose, to anyone else's eyes, it didn't have much to recommend it. But to us, living as we did for the hours when we could close the door on the rest of the world, it had the only things that really mattered—privacy and a bed intended for one, but shared by two.

I was not so naive that I hadn't learned how babies were made and what children were called if their parents weren't married. I knew the stigma such children bore throughout their lives. Yet even armed with all this information, I had given myself to Marco within a week of meeting him, so certain was I that our lives would be forever intertwined. Abandonment, deceit, acts of God or nature or mankind, lay so far outside our realm of possibility that they had no bearing on us.

As I explain that, Carly shakes her head incredulously. "And you never doubted him? It never occurred to you that once you'd left, he'd find someone else?"

"Never."

We were touched with a special magic that lifted us above the rest. Convinced that ours was a love so powerful that nothing could destroy it, I had ventured so far beyond the boundaries of propriety that, had I been discovered, I'd have been ruined. A social outcast, ostracized by "nice" girls and their families.

That's what we were in those days, I tell her. "Girls," paraded before suitable young men and taken by the highest bidder. And our chastity, along with our bloodlines, determined how much we were worth. Not until we sent out engraved cards announcing that *Mrs. Charles So-and-So* is at home, followed by the date and a prestigious address, were we entitled to call ourselves "women."

No pedestrian *Mrs.* for me, though. I would be Signora Marco Paretti, wife of the well-known, well-respected architect. I would live in Fiesole, the hilltop town north of Florence, in a house my husband had designed especially for us and our children.

All this and more comprised my future. For now, though, we had just this one night together in our secret hideaway, and then we'd have to say goodbye.

As soon as I stepped into the room, I saw that Marco had been there earlier. Freesias were arranged in the vase which, previously, had held daisies. Rose petals lay scattered over the bed. A bottle of Chianti and two glasses stood on the small table under the window.

"Tonight we make memories which will carry us through the coming weeks," Marco whispered, content for the moment to hold my hands and look into my eyes.

I started to cry, the beauty of the moment, of his love for me, colliding horribly with the desolation filling my soul. He pulled me close. I realized then that he was crying, too. Great, silent, helpless shudders racked his body.

We clung to each other blindly, and the heat of desire fed on our emotions and burned away everything but the need to fuse our bodies, our hearts, our minds, to give to each other everything we were, everything we had.

We held back nothing. We simply loved each other, deeply, intimately. I heard myself moan and beg in ways that, before, would have left me too embarrassed ever to face him again.

But not that night. That night, I was shameless in my greed. Nothing lay beyond the pale for either of us. Touching, tasting, scrutinizing inch by inch, using words never uttered in polite society—such were the means by which we stitched together the love that had to be strong enough to survive separation.

Not that I share such intimate details with my granddaughter, of course. They belong to Marco and me.

Too soon, first light filtered through the open window. We dressed, fumbling with our clothes as if we could delay the inevitable. But there was no postponing time. A nearby church sounded five o'clock. In four hours, the taxi would come to take my aunt, my cousin and me to the train station. By the next afternoon, I would be in England; a week from then, in America, with over three thousand miles separating me from him.

At the door, I turned for one last glimpse of our hideaway. At the crushed rose petals and the tangle of sheets on the bed. At the half-empty bottle of Chianti. At the freesias perfuming the room with their scent. I knew then that I would never again smell roses or freesias, never again taste the red wine of Tuscany, and not be assailed by the poignant sadness of that moment.

When I returned to our *pensione,* Genevieve snuck down to let me in. "You're cutting it fine," she scolded. "Momma's up already. You're lucky she didn't knock on

our door to make sure we're awake." Then, seeing that I'd
been crying, she hugged me and said, "Don't mind me,
Anna. You're back now, and she's none the wiser. Come
and wash your face with cold water, or she'll wonder why
your eyes are so red."

Her kindness started my tears flowing again. "It nearly
killed me to leave him, Genevieve."

"Don't dwell on that," she said briskly. "Instead concentrate on when you'll see him again."

"Months from now," I wailed, stumbling over our luggage.

In fact, I saw him just a few hours later, at the railroad
station. I was about to board our train when I felt a hand
at my elbow. "*Posso aiutarla, signorina?* May I help you?"

For a moment, I closed my eyes, afraid I was halluci-
nating. But the warmth in his voice, in his touch, were all
too real and left me trembling. "Thank you," I stam-
mered. "*Grazie.*"

"*Prego.*" Marco squeezed my arm in secret intimacy,
smiled into my eyes, and in a low voice added, "*Ti amo,
la mia bella.* Hurry back. I don't want to be apart from you
a day longer than necessary."

"Thank you, young man. We can manage quite well,"
my aunt declared, regarding him suspiciously from the top
step into the train.

"*Si, signora. Buon viaggio.*"

"What was that about?" she sniffed, when we'd found
our seats.

"He wished us a safe journey, that's all," Genevieve
replied for me, because I couldn't speak. I was too busy
pressing my nose to the window and watching him fade
into the distance as the train pulled out of the station.

Aunt Patricia hoisted her bosom into place. "Foreigners! I don't trust them one iota. You girls might be sorry to leave Europe behind, but I can't wait to set foot on American soil again."

The grand tour had come to an end, and so had my idyll. As the train thundered north through Switzerland and into France, rumblings of war brought me back to a reality unlike anything I'd experienced before. Suddenly Marco's political leanings, which he'd hinted at in passing and then casually, as if they were of no great consequence, assumed a frightening dimension.

I recalled that he and his father were outspoken critics of Benito Mussolini, Italy's Fascist dictator and that sometimes, on those evenings when he wasn't with me, Marco attended partisan rallies. I might have been shielded from much of the news, but even I recognized that although the sun shone on Florence and turned the River Arno into a swath of blue silk flowing smoothly under the city's bridges, a dark underbelly existed beneath the ancient calm of the Uffizi and Pitti Palace.

"Well, no need to make yourself sick over that," Genevieve told me, as the boat train approached Southampton. "If you must find something to keep you awake at night, worry about Hitler."

But optimist though she was, Genevieve couldn't help noticing the subdued atmosphere aboard the *Queen Mary* any more than I could. The luxury remained intact, but the laughter flowed less freely, and the young men who'd previously flirted with us on the dance floor now assumed a more solemn bearing.

"It's not very promising over there," they said, referring to the way events were shaping up in Germany. "They'll be up to their necks in it before much longer."

Over there. Synonymous with Europe and war, the term was on everyone's lips, echoing along the Promenade Deck and infiltrating such exclusive retreats as the Verandah Grill. She tried to hide it, but Genevieve wasn't immune to its aura of foreboding. "Not that we have anything to worry about," she insisted when the Statue of Liberty rose up against the skyline and the tugs towed our ship to its berth in New York harbor. "Regardless of what happens *over there,* America won't be involved."

But Italy might be, I thought fearfully.

My parents were waiting at the dock. "We're so relieved to have you home," my mother cried, enveloping me in a hug that squeezed the breath from my lungs. "Your father and I have been frantic these past few days. We were so afraid you'd be stranded in England."

"That wouldn't have happened," Aunt Patricia said. "I kept our passports and tickets on my person at all times."

"But you must have heard," my father told us gravely. "This was likely the *Queen Mary*'s final run as a commercial passenger ship. On September first, just a day after you set sail from Southampton, Germany invaded Poland. On the third, Great Britain, France, Australia and New Zealand declared war on Germany."

The news had reached us, but we hadn't wanted to believe it. Unutterably dismayed, I asked, "How long before it's over?"

He shook his head. "Who's to say? It could be months— or years. It all depends on that madman, Hitler, and how soon they're able to put a stop to him over there."

Over there... Marco was over there, and I was here.

"You look faint, darling," my mother said, stroking my face lovingly. "Were you seasick?"

"No," I managed to say. "It's the shock of hearing that countries we just visited are at war—except for Italy. It's not involved, is it?"

"Not yet," my father said. "But I suspect it will be, before long. Thank God you're home safe is all I can say. For your mother and me, the worst is over."

But it wasn't over, not by a long shot. Although I couldn't begin to guess its extent, the worst was yet to come....

"If talking about it upset you, Gran, you don't have to go on," Carly says urgently, but I shake my head, knowing I must because I'm caught up in a web of memories that won't let me go.

"You have a letter from Italy, Anna," my mother announced, one morning when I came down to breakfast. She flipped over the envelope, checking for a return address. "From an M. Paretti. Someone you met over there, obviously."

"Yes," I said, studiously avoiding her gaze. "A friend. We promised we'd keep in touch."

I'd been home nearly two weeks. Although the skies remained clear, the days were growing shorter, the nights cooler and the maples turning color. Fall had always been my favorite season, until this year when each hour was a purgatory to be endured.

Every day, the news from Europe grew more ominous. On September 10, Canada had joined the Allies. The war had reached North American shores, after all. But Italy was still uninvolved, and the sight of that flimsy blue envelope with its foreign stamp, the first from Marco, sent such a wash of relief over me that I thought I might be sick.

My mother watched me, smiling. "Aren't you going to read it?"

"Later." I moved away, busying myself with the dishes our housekeeper had set on the sideboard in the breakfast room. "After I've eaten."

But the bacon and hotcakes turned my stomach. "I hardly call that eating," my father remarked, eyeing my slice of toast and cup of coffee as he rose from the table. "What happened to your appetite?"

"I'm not very hungry lately."

"That's not normal for a girl your age." He paused long enough to drop a kiss on my head and another on my mother's cheek. "Perhaps you should take her to see Dr. Grant, Isabelle. Could be she needs a tonic."

"Your father's right," my mother observed after he'd gone. "Lately you're not yourself at all, Anna. You're pale and listless. I hope you didn't pick up some sort of disease when you were away."

For a moment, I was tempted to tell her that I had, and it was fatal—that I'd fallen desperately in love with a handsome Italian and was heartsick at being separated from him.

"Travel can be exhausting," she continued sympathetically. "Your aunt Patricia remarked just yesterday that she's still not back to normal. She mentioned, too, that you tired easily when you were away, even though you and Genevieve were never late getting to bed. I suppose, if the truth be known, the pair of you spent half the night talking when you should've been sleeping, and now it's catching up with you."

"That's probably it," I mumbled, ashamed not that I'd spent so many nights in Marco's arms, but that I was lying about it and perhaps hiding an even bigger secret, one that would devastate her should my suspicions prove correct. "Don't worry, Momma. There really isn't anything wrong with me that time won't cure." In a fever of impatience to read my letter, I added with false cheer, "I'm sure you have a million things to do besides watching me eat toast, so don't feel you have to keep me company."

"Then I won't, because you're right. I do have a full day ahead. Will you be home for lunch?"

"No. I'm meeting Genevieve at the yacht club."

"I'll see you at dinner then. Have fun, honey, and give her a kiss for me."

The door had barely closed behind her when I used my butter spreader to slit open the pale blue envelope. My pulse hammered erratically as I extracted the folded sheets of paper and smoothed them flat. Did he still love me? Had distance made his heart grow fonder, or was I fading in his mind now that I was out of sight?

I OPEN THE FOLDER on the table in front of me, extract the first page of the letter and show it to Carly. Then I begin to read:

Firenze
September 4, 1939
Anna, my love,
It has only been a few days since I watched the train to Paris take you away from me, but even in so short a time, the world as we knew it is forever changed. The war people have talked about for months has

finally come to pass and I, who should fear for the future of my own country more than ever before, care only about you.

How glad I am, *tesoro,* that you are safe in America. Yet how lonely I am without you. I consider myself a brave enough man, prepared to fight for what I believe is right and just, but courage is no match for the desolation I feel at knowing we shall be apart much longer than we expected.

Adolf Hitler has changed the face of Europe. Even if it was possible, you must not think of returning to Italy until he and his Nazi thugs have been crushed. The danger is too great. To live without you a few months more than I expected will be difficult. To risk living without you forever, impossible. You have become my life, and I ask nothing more of God than for the day to come when I wake up beside you every morning, and hold you close in my arms each night.

The news here is disturbing, *amore mio.* Only the most naive among us believe that Mussolini has our country's best interests at heart. He is corrupt and evil. If he can further his own ambitions by allying himself with Adolf Hitler, he will do so without a moment's thought for the ultimate cost to Italy. Those opposed to his regime no longer have the right to voice their opinions openly. In the last week alone, one of our group here in Firenze was "interrogated" by government officials for eight hours. He is recovering in hospital. A second has been thrown in prison. Two others have disappeared. Consequently our partisan rallies now take place in secret.

I am desolate at what all this implies, but as long as you are safe, my memories of you will help me survive whatever restrictions or hardships I must face. If my English were more fluent, I might find it easier to express the depth of emotion you inspire in me. But it is not, and so all I can say is I love you, my Anna. I miss you. And I count the hours until we can be together again. Until then, know that I carry you deep in my heart. You are with me always.

Forever yours,

Marco

"I devoured every word that day, Carly," I tell her, tracing my finger over each letter, as if, by doing so, I could touch him. "I realized I was crying when my tears blurred the ink and left great wet spots on the paper. Look, Carly." I point at several places. "All these years later, you can see how faded some words are."

She bends her head close to look. Nods. Touches the paper, ever so softly.

"I was so afraid for him," I continue, "but I believed in him. He was brave and strong, he was alive, and most of all, he loved me still. I told myself that as long as those things remained constant, it would be enough."

Carly covers my hand with hers. "But it wasn't, was it, Gran?"

"No, it wasn't, because nothing remains constant in war except death and destruction, not merely of cities and innocent men, women and children, but of the hopes and dreams of those who somehow manage to survive."

CHAPTER FOUR

As SEPTEMBER of 1939 progressed, mellow with sunshine during the day and sharp with a hint of frost at night, Marco and I wrote daily, without waiting for each other's replies. But where I hid my fears, especially the one I had increasing reason to think was the legacy of our weeks together, and filled my letters with plans for our future, his took an increasingly dark turn.

Sifting through my letters, I choose one to illustrate my point.

There is a stillness here in Firenze, he wrote toward the end of the fourth week. *A sort of calm before the storm. Mussolini's Blackshirts are on every street corner, watchful for any hint of insurrection. Their motto, Me ne frego, means I do not give a damn, and its message begins to make itself felt in every quarter. As a result, neighbors keep to themselves and are careful in what they say. Doors open cautiously after dark to admit a stealthy visitor, and close quickly again, before he can be recognized. Shutters are drawn across windows.*

Hitler's influence is felt ever more keenly in our country. The fellow who lives on the floor above mine, a Jewish scholar and a gentle, harmless man, was taken by the

Blackshirts two days ago. There has been no word of him since and when a friend went to inquire for him at militia headquarters, he was warned not to interfere in matters of the state unless he, too, wished to jeopardize his liberty. Once upon a time, I believed that all a man needed to direct the course of his own destiny was honor, integrity and the courage to stand by his ideals. I no longer believe these are enough. We are learning to keep our heads down and confide only in trusted friends—although, sadly, they, too, sometimes betray us for sins either real or imagined. Even to you, my dearest love, I dare not speak too freely of my activities, for fear that my letter might fall into the wrong hands. All I can say without reservation is that I love you with my whole heart and that will never change, no matter what comes next.

...no matter what comes next... These words filled me with a festering dread made worse by the fact that, as October dragged by with its blasts of cold rain, his letters grew less frequent and ever more somber. They almost prepared me for the shocking news that his father, an influential Florentine businessman and outspoken critic of Mussolini's repressive Fascist regime, had been executed on September 30.

Knowing how close he and his father had been, I ached for Marco and longed to hold him in my arms and comfort him with my love. Instead I had to be content with written words which, however much I tried, never adequately conveyed all that lay in my heart. I tried to hide how afraid I was for him, but the possibility that he might follow his father's fate was never far from my mind.

"What happened to Signor Paretti is horrible, but Marco

will see it for the warning it is, and not take any chances with his own safety," Genevieve said, when I confided my fears to her. "He's got too much to live for. After all, he's got you."

Brian, the one other person who knew of my love affair, also did his best to comfort me. Although he was attending Rhode Island College in Kingston during the week, working on his graduate degree in mathematics, he came home most weekends and always made a point of calling on me and inviting me to take long walks with him.

Loyal friend that he was, he let me unburden myself without fear of being overheard. Our parents, though, misinterpreting his motives, exchanged pleased glances and smiled in tacit approval of what they perceived to be his courtship.

"This war won't last forever, Anna. Everything'll return to normal once it's over, you'll see," he consoled me one brisk, windy day toward the end of the month.

I wished I could believe him, but my life was spinning out of control, and for me "normal" was as much a part of my past as my innocence. Marco's infrequent letters were my anchor during those dark days, the one tenuous link that saved me from absolute despair.

When they suddenly ceased and my last letter to him was returned, with *No longer at this address* scrawled in Italian across the envelope, I was in despair. Despite the risk of arousing my parents' curiosity, if not their outright suspicion, I sent a telegram to Rudolfo Nesta, Marco's good friend and colleague whom I'd met once or twice in Florence, begging him for news.

His reply came two days later, in the middle of a Saturday afternoon.

When the telegram boy arrived on his bike, Brian and I were at the foot of the long driveway leading from my home to the road, so we were able to intercept him before he reached the front door. Hands shaking, I tore at the yellow envelope, desperate to get at what lay inside. Praying it was good news, perhaps even a message from Marco himself telling me not to worry and that all was well. And if neither of those things, then at least a sliver of hope—anything except what it took me seconds to read. To this day, I remember every word.

Two weeks ago Blackshirts invaded house where Marco spent evening with companions STOP None seen or heard from since STOP Fear the worst STOP Regret being bearer of bad news STOP Rudolfo STOP

I remember crying out and my legs giving way, then knew nothing until I found myself sitting on a fallen log, several yards along a tree-shaded path that led to the greenhouses at the rear of our property. A seagull's forlorn cry broke the silence. The air smelled of damp and dying things. Overhead, the leaves on the maples gleamed red as blood.

"Your grandfather crouched beside me, Carly, one arm around my shoulders, the telegram in his other hand. I looked at him, wanting reassurance, wanting him to tell me, in that calm, rational manner of his, that I shouldn't assume the worst. I wanted him to give me the hope I couldn't find for myself."

He had none to offer. His blue eyes bruised with pain, he said quietly, "I'm so sorry, Anna."

"Oh, Gran!" Carly's voice quavers with genuine sympathy. "You must've been heartbroken."

"Yes. But some grief, I learned that day, defies outward

expression," I tell her. It simply consumes, orchestrating a person to its own merciless rhythm of silent, roaring blackness. Tears might have offered a blessed, albeit temporary, relief but my eyes remained dry. My mind flash-froze, emblazoned with Rudolfo's message. For a while, I felt neither the chill fall air on my face, nor the warm clasp of Brian's hand. The only part of me unaffected was my damnable heart which continued to function, denying the release I craved from this living hell.

I have no idea how long we sat there. An hour or more, I suspect, because the light had started to dim under the trees when Brian stirred and, chafing my hands between his palms, murmured, "Tell me what can I do, Anna."

I shook my head. "Nothing. Go home. Let me be."

I didn't add, *I want to die,* but he read my mind all too accurately.

"Anything but that," he said, and drew me to my feet. "Let's walk for a while. You can't face your parents in your present state."

Back then, we lived close by Easton's Pond where swans and mallards drifted serenely, untouched by human tragedy. A ten-minute stroll along its banks led to The Cliff Walk, with its magnificent views of the Atlantic. Dangerous in places, with sheer drops to the rocks below, it was not a place for the unwary—or the hopelessly bereft. Mindful of that, Brian stationed himself between me and the edge and kept my arm firmly tucked beneath his.

Clouds had rolled in, leaving the sky a sullen gunmetal-gray except for a streak of gold where the sun had set. The wind was strong, whipping the waves to an angry froth as they hurtled toward shore. It made the breath snag in my throat and stung the tears suddenly dripping down my face.

Noticing, Brian stopped and, without a word, turned me toward him and buried my face in his shoulder. The rough tweed of his jacket muffled my sobs and soaked up my tears. I didn't care if other people passed by and recognized us in the fading light. The world Marco and I had created was no more, and nothing else mattered.

Brian stood there patiently until the worst had passed, then took a clean handkerchief from his breast pocket and mopped my face. "Do you want me to take you home, honey?"

"No," I said, on an exhausted hiccup. "I can't, not yet. I have to think about…"

About what to do next.

"To Genevieve's, then?"

I clutched at the idea as if it were a life preserver. Genevieve was my soul sister, and I'd never needed her more than I did at that moment. She'd met Marco, had seen how he cherished me. He was more than just a name to her. He had a face, a smile, a voice, a laugh. She'd understand. But… "What if she's not home and Aunt Patricia sees us? She'll guess I've been crying. What do I tell her?"

"Good point. We'll go to that small hotel on Bridge Street. I'll phone her, and if she's home, get her to meet us there."

We left Cliff Walk at Narragansett Avenue and went into the town proper, entering the hotel lobby to call Genevieve. She arrived a short while later in the family's chauffeur-driven Packard. Flinging her arms around me in a tight hug, she said, "I stopped by to tell your parents we decided to meet for dinner and not to expect you home until later."

We were shown to a quiet table in the corner of the

dimly lit dining room. A blessing, because seeing each other had us both in tears, and Brian's hands were full coping with us. He ordered a meal only he tackled with any appetite. Genevieve picked at her chicken breast, and I barely touched my poached fish.

"You have to eat, Anna," she scolded, when I pushed aside my plate. "You'll make yourself ill if you don't, and Marco would never want that."

"I can't."

"Why not?"

"I'm not hungry."

"That's what you said at lunch, the other day. Remember?"

How could I forget, when I'd been sick to my stomach for days? But I'd tried hard to deny the reason for my nausea in the hope that, if my suspicions were correct, Marco and I would deal with it together. I knew now that that would never happen.

My despair must have shown on my face because Genevieve leaned across the table and pinned me with a probing gaze. "There's something else, isn't there? What is it?"

I couldn't carry the burden alone a moment longer. "I think I'm pregnant," I blurted out, finally giving words to the misgivings that had haunted me for weeks.

Brian sat as if he'd been turned to stone. But Genevieve closed her eyes and let out a sigh. "I was afraid that was it. Oh, Anna, what are you going to do?"

"I don't know."

"Whatever you decide, you can count on us." She fixed a fierce hazel glare on Brian. "Can't she?"

"Every step of the way." Slowly he rubbed his jaw, a

habit that meant his mind was sorting through the facts and establishing priorities. "Had you told Marco?"

I shook my head, enough to send yet more tears splashing down my face. "I wanted to be sure before I said anything. He was already dealing with so much...."

"Don't cry, sweetie." Drawing her chair closer to mine, Genevieve gripped my hand. "There are things we can do. A girl at school—"

"Let's not get ahead of ourselves and start assuming the worst," Brian interrupted. "You've been under a lot of pressure lately, Anna. What you think are symptoms of a baby on the way might be nothing more than stress. Have you seen a doctor?"

"No," I wailed.

"Then that's the logical next step."

"I can't go to Dr. Grant. He's known me all my life." I gulped, the enormity of my plight hitting home with a vengeance. "I'm still a minor. He'd have to tell my parents."

Their treasured only child pregnant out of wedlock? It would kill them!

"We'll find another doctor," Genevieve said, doing her best to shore up my spirits. "We'll go to another town where no one will recognize us."

But the news from Italy, coupled with my certainty that I hadn't mistaken my symptoms, left me past all hope. "Where?" I whimpered.

"Wakefield," Brian announced. "It's just a few miles down the road from Kingston. We have a Visitors' Day at the college on Tuesday, and I was going to ask if the two of you wanted to come."

Genevieve frowned. "But won't your mother and father be there?"

"No. This is mostly for younger people—a chance for us to show off what we're up to and for future students to have a look around and see what the place has to offer. The instructors make themselves available in the morning, and we're expected to direct visitors to the lecture halls, but there's a football game in the afternoon. No one's going to miss me if I don't show up for that."

"And a doctor?"

"There's bound to be one in Wakefield. Let me set up an appointment and you concentrate on getting there. You shouldn't have any problem, now that regular bus service runs from Newport. Tell me when you'll be getting in and I'll meet you."

Genevieve eyed me apprehensively. "Three more days. Think you can hold on that long, Anna?"

What she meant was, could I go through the motions and continue fooling my parents into believing all was well with me when, in fact, my heart was breaking and my future loomed blacker than night.

"I have to," I said. "They don't deserve this."

But if the doctor confirmed what I instinctively knew to be the case, I was merely postponing the inevitable. Eventually, either I'd have to tell them the truth or my body would do it for me.

TOO IMMERSED in grief and worry to care about practicalities, I followed blindly as Genevieve and Brian steered me through the ordeal of the medical appointment on Tuesday afternoon. A borrowed wedding ring and a bogus husband was all it took.

"Wexley," Brian stated firmly when the nurse at the desk asked our name. "Mr. and Mrs. Brian Wexley. My wife has a three-o'clock appointment with Dr. Reese."

I cringed at yet another lie designed to shield me from the consequences of my rash behavior. Genevieve had "borrowed" her late grandmother's plain gold ring from her mother's jewelry case, and it hung around the third finger of my left hand like a lead weight. My cousin's last words, before Brian and I entered the small clinic, had been, "Stop looking so furtive. They'll think you're Rhode Island's answer to Bonnie and Clyde!"

But that infamous pair had been killed in 1934. A vastly preferable state, I thought morosely, to the one in which I now found myself. A kind of numbness had carried me through the last couple of days, but it was wearing thin as the moment of truth approached.

Within minutes, the nurse beckoned to me. "Dr. Reese will see you first, Mrs. Wexley. Your husband may join you later."

The indignity of what came next—me stripped naked and covered by a white sheet, my feet nesting in cold metal stirrups, my legs spread wide, and a man I'd never seen before probing at my body—mortified me, but what couldn't be avoided had to be endured, and all too soon the verdict was in.

"About nine weeks along, I'd say," the doctor informed me, restoring my modesty by pulling the sheet over me before turning to the door. "Get dressed, my dear, then we'll pass the good news to your husband and discuss the regimen I'd like you to follow over the next several months."

An hour later, as I sat in a tearoom, flanked by my friends, it struck me how seriously they'd compromised their own reputations in order to preserve mine. Brian, especially, had taken a huge risk. "You gave them your real name," I gasped, horrified.

The hint of a smile touched his mouth. "I felt 'Smith' didn't possess quite enough cachet."

"But they'll assume you're the baby's father!"

"Yes."

"What about you?" Genevieve asked me. "How do you feel, now that the pregnancy's confirmed, I mean?"

"Torn. Overwhelmed." I dreaded what lay ahead. I could no longer put off the inevitable. My parents would have to be told. If they didn't disown me, they'd send me away to give birth in secret, then insist I have the baby adopted. But this was all I had left of Marco. How could I ever part with this child?

"You don't have to go through with the pregnancy, you know," Genevieve said in a low voice. "There are certain…clinics in New York or Boston where people in your situation can be helped. It's a matter of finding the right name—"

"No," Brian interrupted flatly. "They're illegal and unsafe. Women die in those places."

She rounded on him, concern for me making her shrill. "You have a better idea, do you?"

"Yes. Anna and I will get married."

Dumbfounded, I stared at him. "You can't be serious!"

"Why not? We're both single and unattached. My prospects are good. I'm twenty-four and ready to settle down, and you need a husband. No doubt people will talk and add up dates when your condition becomes obvious, but they'll assume the baby's mine and that's what matters. Based on our lifelong friendship and the fondness we have for each other, I'd say that all adds up to a pretty compelling reason to plan a wedding as soon as possible."

I pause in my story, turning to Carly. "He was offering me an easy solution, and the temptation to take him up on it was huge. Although he was nothing like Marco, your grandfather, Carly, was the sort of man any woman would be proud to call her husband, and believe me when I say I was well aware of that fact. He was tall, strong and good-looking. An avid sailor, crack golfer and former high school basketball star. More than that, he was kind and generous and intelligent."

She nods mutely and I go on.

We shared a similar background, Brian and I, and if I'd never spent a summer in Italy, I might very well have married him anyway. But "I can't let you do this," I protested. "You don't deserve to be smeared with my scandal."

"Does your baby deserve to be labeled a bastard, Anna? Consider that before you turn me down."

His observation brought home the wider implications of my situation. Those other options—an illegal abortion, or adoption—were out of the question. How could I deny my baby, when his father had taught me that nothing is shameful or forbidden in the expression of true love? Yet to subject a child to the shame of illegitimacy was equally unacceptable.

Still, I made one last stab at resistance. "What about our parents? Won't they be suspicious?"

"Don't worry about them," Brian said with a laugh. "They've already got us halfway down the aisle. They'll be happy to push us the rest of the way."

"It would be the ideal solution," Genevieve murmured.

Brian squeezed my hand. "And definitely best for the baby."

Suddenly, from the ashes of my dreams, a tiny miracle presented itself. Part of Marco was growing inside me. I owed it to him to give his child the best possible life, and because of Brian's generosity and decency, I was in a position to do so.

"You don't have to decide right away," he said, taking my silence for uncertainty. "Think it over, and let me know when I come home on the weekend."

But making up my mind on the spot, I said, "I don't need to wait that long. I'll marry you, Brian, and I promise you now that you'll never regret it. I'll do everything in my power to make you happy."

His smile suggested I'd done him the world's biggest favor. No one watching would have guessed that ours would be a marriage of convenience. "Then start making plans. I'll speak to your father on Saturday."

I never learned exactly what transpired between my father and Brian that next weekend. They remained in the library quite a while, their voices an indistinct rumble beyond the thick oak door. But by Sunday, I was wearing an engagement ring and that night, our two families celebrated our upcoming wedding with dinner at the yacht club.

Thankfully my nausea wasn't too severe, and I wasn't showing yet. My clothes, though, didn't fit as easily as they once had and if I didn't want to be escorted down the aisle with my burgeoning midriff half-hidden behind a massive bouquet, we had little time to lose.

"We thought two weeks from now, on the seventh of November," Brian said, when asked about a wedding date.

"But that's far too soon!" my mother objected. "Why, I'm not sure we can even get a decent wedding dress by then, let alone a place to hold a reception. What's the rush?"

"The holiday season's coming up, and that's always busy," he explained. Then, with charming diffidence added, "And I'm an impatient groom. I don't want to wait until the new year. Anna might change her mind about taking me on as a husband."

"We'd prefer something quiet and intimate anyway," I said, playing my part as eager bride. "With the situation in Europe as bad as it is, a big, splashy wedding seems rather tasteless."

I'd effectively shifted attention away from us and back to the ever-present topic of the war. "You've got a point," my future father-in-law agreed. "It's just a matter of time before America's in the thick of it, so you might as well enjoy yourselves while you still can."

I substituted an aquamarine silk suit with a matching hat for the long white gown and bridal veil I'd always imagined I'd wear on my wedding day. Genevieve, in dove-gray, was my only attendant.

Brian and I were married in my parents' drawing room, in front of a handful of guests, with a pale November sun shining through the windows. After a champagne lunch, he and I slipped away for a two-day honeymoon in Connecticut.

Ironically I was able to continue as Dr. Reese's patient because, for a wedding present, our parents bought us the house in Wakefield. We were very lucky. If they had questions about the haste with which Brian and I had rushed into marriage, they chose not to say them aloud. We were, to all intents and purposes, a blissfully happy couple, beginning a long life together. No one but Brian knew how often I cried myself to sleep at night.

CHAPTER FIVE

A FLIGHT ATTENDANT came by to spread linen place mats over their tables and offer drinks. "They're getting ready to serve dinner, Gran, and you're losing your voice," Carly said, glad of an excuse to halt the story before she said something she'd regret.

Her earlier resentment had come flooding back, burying any fledgling sympathy she'd felt for Anna's blighted love affair. Her grandpa Brian was a hero in his own right and deserved better than to be another man's stand-in. As for Marco Paretti, he had a lot to answer for, seducing an innocent girl and leaving her pregnant. Anna might have been a virgin when they met, but Carly would bet her last dollar the same couldn't be said about him. He was smooth, though; she'd grant him that.

"A glass of white wine, please," she told the flight attendant. The mood she was in right then, she could have downed a whole bottle and it wouldn't have numbed her indignation. How she was going to stomach a whole summer with the man who'd stolen her grandmother's heart and served her grandfather the leftovers, she couldn't imagine.

But the in-flight meal couldn't last forever, and before

long Anna was rooting through her stack of letters, clearly impatient to pick up where she'd left off.

Resigned, Carly settled in for the next installment.

I HIDE A SMILE, aware that I haven't made a fan of my granddaughter quite yet. The mutinous set of her mouth reminds me of her mother when she was a teenager.

"I'd discovered a gem in Brian," I begin.

Although unfailingly tender with me, not once during those first few weeks did he press me to consummate our marriage. My health and the well-being of my baby were his primary concerns. Gradually, though, acceptance of what I couldn't change softened the raw edges of my grief a little, and by Christmas I was prompted by both guilt and gratitude to become in fact the wife I was in name. Difficult though it might be, I knew I'd have to make the first overtures.

Our house looked very festive, with a large wreath on the front door, a Norfolk pine in the living room and evergreen swags along the mantelpieces. On Christmas Eve, after we'd placed our gifts under the tree, we went upstairs and, as was our habit, prepared for bed separately in the privacy of the bathroom. Neither of us had ever seen the other naked. That night, though, instead of putting on my usual flannel nightgown with the long sleeves and high neck, I appeared in the bedroom wearing the silky, rather naughty gown Genevieve had given me as part of my trousseau. By then I was well into my sixteenth week, and despite the tragedy that had marked its beginning, pregnancy agreed with me. My skin glowed and my hair fell thick and lustrous to my shoulders. Genevieve's gift was made for a woman with the kind of lush curves I now possessed.

Brian was already in bed, reading with the pillows propped at his back, but when he glanced up and saw me, the book fell from his hands and slid to the floor.

Climbing in beside him, I placed my hand on his chest. "You seem surprised," I said—a vast understatement, considering he was almost glassy-eyed with shock, "but it's about time, wouldn't you say?"

A somewhat ambiguous invitation, no doubt, but he understood what I was really saying. "Are you sure, Anna?"

Just briefly, the last time I'd made love nibbled at my mind before I managed to shut out the memory. "Very," I said, and slowly undid the buttons on his pajama jacket. "You are my husband, Brian."

Our lovemaking was slow and very sweet. He was nervous, and endearingly clumsy because of it. "I've never done this before," he muttered, lifting the hem of my gown with trembling fingers.

I couldn't say the same, but I wasn't any sort of expert, either, so we stumbled on together, discovering each other in the dark because we were too bashful to leave the light on. And for the first time in my marriage—perhaps even in my entire life—I gave of myself unselfishly, caring more about pleasing someone else than my own needs.

After, we lay with our hands joined. "Merry Christmas," I whispered.

"Merry Christmas, Mrs. Wexley," he said. Then, after a pause, "How are you doing *really?*"

For a moment I was tempted to take the question at face value and tell him I felt wonderful. But he wasn't asking about our lovemaking, and if I had to identify the greatest strength in our marriage, it was that we never lied to each other. Now was not the time to start.

"Some days are better than others," I admitted, "but it's becoming easier, and I have you to thank for that. I don't know what I'd do without you."

"You'll never have to find out, honey," he said. "I want you to be happy again, and I'm willing to do whatever it takes to make that happen. I love you."

"I love you, too," I said, and it was true. That it wasn't the same sort of love I'd known with Marco didn't make it any less real.

He reached down and boldly stroked the slightly convex dome of my abdomen. "When are we going to come clean with our folks about this?"

We were spending Christmas Day with both families at his parents' house. "Perhaps tomorrow would be appropriate—a sort of bonus gift. Apart from anything else, we can't put off telling them much longer."

"I'm surprised they haven't already noticed," Brian remarked.

But I'd been wearing concealing clothes, and also I wasn't very big for four months, which had been a concern until Dr. Reese assured me there was no cause for alarm. Our parents probably attributed the reason I was blooming to our wedded bliss.

"Marriage must suit you," my mother had commented just a few days before. "You lost so much weight and seemed so listless after you came back from Europe, and it's good to see you looking more like your old self again. For a while, we were worried that you'd picked up some sort of ailment while you were in Europe."

Would they immediately jump to a different conclusion when we shared the news? I wondered.

Echoing my question, Brian said, "The first thing they'll ask is when the baby's due."

"I know."

Approximately May 31, Dr. Reese had predicted. A scant six months after the wedding, which in itself could lead to unfortunate speculation about who the father might be, since I'd been on the other side of the world when I'd conceived.

"We don't have to be too exact," he suggested. "Let's tell them you're due in the summer and leave it at that. From all I've read, first babies especially don't adhere to a rigid timetable. Just because we happen to know this one's going to be born ahead of schedule doesn't obligate us to share the news with anyone else. Once he puts in an appearance, the excitement of having a grandchild will be all our parents care about."

"But they can count," I said. "Sooner or later, they'll figure out I was pregnant when we got married."

"They're probably already wondering, Anna, considering how we rushed the wedding, but I doubt they'll be so crass as to make an issue of something they can do absolutely nothing about. If they do, though, I'm perfectly prepared to tell them it's none of their business."

One reason I loved my husband was that he took problems I tended to blow out of all proportion and put them in perspective. "This is one lucky baby, that he has you to look out for him," I murmured sleepily.

He pulled me closer and tucked the covers more snugly around us. "It's not a matter of luck. It's about doing whatever you can for the people you care about."

As he predicted, our parents were thrilled at the idea of a grandchild, and if they were indeed suspicious about the timing, they chose to ignore it.

Once the news was out, the baby became the favorite topic of conversation, almost overshadowing the worsening situation in Europe. Our mothers vied to see who could knit faster, then joined forces on shopping sprees to Boston, coming home loaded with parcels. By February, I had enough infant clothes to outfit an orphanage. My parents bought the crib; Brian's, the baby carriage. My father rescued from the attic the antique cradle I'd slept in as a newborn and applied a fresh coat of varnish.

Brian put in long days at the college during the early part of the new year, hoping to complete his studies by the end of the spring session. During the hours he was gone, I kept busy setting up the nursery and fulfilling my social obligations as a married woman.

Helped by my mother's housekeeper, I learned to cook, and tried to have the evening meal prepared when Brian came home. We ate by candlelight, in the dining room, using our everyday china and silver-plate cutlery. On weekends, when we often entertained, I brought out the fine china and the sterling.

"Were you really happy during those early months, Gran?" Carly asks hopefully.

"In all honesty, darling girl, no, I was not. Too often at night, Marco stole in while I slept. My dreams—sometimes painful, sometimes glorious but always vivid—took me hostage. I relived those precious weeks we'd shared, hearing his voice, seeing his face. Some days, I'd wake up smiling and happy—until reality intruded and made me cry."

What I don't add is that other times, the dreams were so powerful that my body betrayed me. Carly didn't need to hear that I had, in effect, committed adultery in my sleep. Once, I opened my eyes in the middle of the night to find the bedside lamp turned on and Brian shaking me, his face drawn with anxiety. "What is it?" he whispered. "Are you in pain, honey?"

"No," I said, struggling awake. "Why do you ask?"

"You were whimpering and shuddering in your sleep."

Not surprising. Secret parts of me quivered still from Marco's ghostly touch.

Unable to meet my husband's gaze, I closed my eyes again. "A bad dream."

"About what?"

"I don't remember."

Yes, I lied, because telling him the truth would've hurt him even more than my dreams hurt me. Sex didn't play a major role in our marriage. We made love regularly but not often, and I never experienced with him the ecstasy I'd had with Marco. Intimacy with Brian was pleasant. With Marco, it had been magnificent.

"But if I wasn't completely happy," I assure Carly, "I was not miserably unhappy, either."

As winter melted into spring, I stopped wishing for miracles, and instead gave thanks for the man who'd saved my good name by marrying me, and who went to such pains to take care of me and the child I carried that was not his.

In April, Brian graduated with top honors and was offered a position as lecturer at the college. "Convenient, don't you agree?" he said, patting my bulging midriff. "Babies, I'm told, are expensive."

Never having had to worry about money, I smiled. "We can afford this one, though."

"We're able to afford a great many things, Anna," he said soberly, "but we live in uncertain times. So many men lost fortunes in the Depression, and with the war in Europe escalating, who's to say what the future might bring?"

"Well, we have our trust funds."

"I refuse to dip into yours, and mine is our rainy-day account, which is why I'm so grateful I have a secure job so I can finally provide properly for my family. I'm well aware that if it weren't for our parents' generosity, we wouldn't be living so comfortably in such a fine house."

So that was it! We'd both enjoyed a privileged upbringing, and it hurt his pride to think he couldn't keep me in the manner to which I'd always been accustomed. Heaving myself out of my chair—in the last month, I'd ballooned in size, although I was still quite small compared to other women attending the clinic—I rose awkwardly on tiptoe and kissed his cheek. "You have done nothing but provide well for me from the day you married me," I told him. "If it weren't for you, I'd be living among strangers in a home for unwed mothers."

MY SON WAS BORN at 4:41 a.m., on June 12, 1940, two days after Italy declared war on Britain and France. He weighed five pounds, three ounces, and this, coupled with his very late arrival, lent some credence to the idea that he was premature. Not that I cared one iota what other people might think of Mrs. Brian Wexley becoming a mother a mere seven months after she got married. All that mattered to me was that he had the requisite number of fingers and toes and, despite his low birth weight, was healthy.

That afternoon, Genevieve showed up in my private room at the hospital, bearing a huge bouquet of flowers for me and a silver rattle for my boy. "Oh, Anna, he's beautiful!" she breathed, peeking at him as he lay in my arms surveying the world.

"He's more than beautiful," I insisted. "He's perfect."

Casting a wary eye around to make sure no one passing by the open door could overhear, she said softly, "He's also the living image of Marco. Look at that black hair—and his mouth! There's nothing of you in him and obviously nothing of Brian."

She wasn't telling me anything I hadn't discovered for myself. The resemblance was startling, but surely remarkable only to someone who'd known Marco. "Except for his blue eyes," I pointed out, latching on to the one noticeable difference.

"All babies start out with blue eyes," she declared. "His will probably turn brown by the time he's six months old. Are you going to call him Mark?"

I shook my head. "Steven, after Brian's grandfather. It's the least I can do. Brian was very touched when I told him."

"He's seen the baby, I take it?"

"Yes. He stopped by this morning before his first class. The red roses on the dresser are from him."

"How was he with this little one?"

I smiled, remembering how proudly he'd marched around the room with Steven, showing him the world beyond the window and telling him all the wonderful things life had in store for him. "He couldn't be more thrilled or excited if…well, you know."

She nodded. "He's a wonderful man, Anna."

"I'm well aware of that," I said.

"What about the grandparents? Have they visited yet?"

"No. I'm expecting them this afternoon."

Right on cue, footsteps sounded in the corridor outside my door and a moment later my mother, mother-in-law and Aunt Patricia flocked into the room, all three laden with flowers and gifts. The grandfathers, I learned, were parking the car.

Genevieve moved aside so they could hold the baby. "Oh my, he's certainly his mommy's little boy," my mother cooed, stroking a gentle finger down his cheek before reluctantly passing him to his other grandmother.

My mother-in-law disagreed. "I beg to differ, Isabelle. I see Brian in him."

"You're both wrong," Aunt Patricia said flatly, when it was her turn.

At that, Genevieve and I exchanged alarmed glances, simultaneously recalling that Aunt Patricia had, in fact, seen Marco at the train station the day we left Florence.

"He has Brian's nose and ears," my aunt decided, subjecting my son to a thorough examination, "and Anna's chin and long fingers. In short, he's exactly what you'd expect—a little bit of both parents…."

Behind their backs, Genevieve grinned and gave me a thumbs-up.

"And," my aunt concluded, "a bit different from both, making him mostly himself, which is exactly as it should be."

The grandfathers arrived shortly after, and we went

through the whole routine again. I was exhausted when the visit ended, and very glad to hand my baby over to the nurse so that I could catch up on my sleep.

We brought him home ten days later. Concerned that I might overdo it, Brian had hired a live-in nanny to help me through those early days. Peggy O'Hannon, a no-nonsense Irish widow in her early fifties and herself the mother of four grown boys, came with impeccable references and took immediate charge.

Steven's weight had dropped to five pounds after his birth. Before we left the hospital, he'd regained the lost ounces and then some, but he was still under six pounds and needed to be nursed every two to three hours. Unfortunately, try though I might, I couldn't keep up with the demand, and the effort to do so was wearing me out.

One day when he was almost a month old, Peggy found both me and him in tears—with him screaming at the top of his lungs. "It doesn't matter what I do, I can't stop his crying," I sobbed.

She plucked Steven from my arms and laid him against her shoulder. The disloyal little beast immediately calmed and began sucking urgently at the side of her neck. "Well, of course you can't, darlin'," she said cheerfully, "because, as I've been telling you for the last week, himself is hungry. Every now and then, we have to supplement what he's getting from you, with a bottle."

"But it says in the book that my milk will dry up if I do that," I wailed.

"At the rate you're going, it'll dry up anyway. An anxious mother makes for an anxious baby. Wipe your eyes now, take a long nap and leave him to me."

I spent a blissful afternoon in bed. Peggy prepared dinner, which I enjoyed in peace with my husband. I didn't see or hear from Steven again until eight o'clock, when she brought him to me to be nursed. By then, my breasts were full and aching. That night, he slept four whole hours before needing to be fed again.

INITIALLY Peggy had come to us for six months, but she remained with us for years, an indispensable part of our household. She taught me how to be a mother and was always there when I needed advice or a helping hand.

Parenthood strengthened the existing bond of affection between Brian and me. He truly loved Steven and never once gave me cause to question his devotion to our son. How could I not love him for that?

In Steven's secure little world, Daddy was the man who, when he arrived home from the college every day, swung him high in the air and made him squeal with glee. It was to Brian's open arms that he tottered on unsteady feet the day he took his first step at thirteen months. The night he came down with an earache, Brian let me sleep and walked the floor with him, then put in a full day's teaching at the college the next day. Brian was the one who took him for his first real haircut.

"That man is clear crazy about his blue-eyed boy," Peggy remarked more than once, and she was right on all counts. Contrary to Genevieve's prediction, Steven's eyes had not turned brown.

Smiling, I turn to Carly. "I became pregnant again in February 1941 and gave birth to your mother that November, just prior to America entering the war, and a few months before your grandfather was commissioned as a captain in the army."

Grace weighed almost eight pounds. As fair as Steven was dark, she was undeniably a Wexley and caused me none of the early grief I'd suffered with my firstborn. By Christmas, she was sleeping through the night.

Steven, meanwhile, had grown into a handsome, sweet-natured boy who adored his baby sister and worried terribly when she cried. "Such a sensitive little mite," Peggy would croon, swooping him onto her lap. "We have to toughen you up, darlin', or the world's going to break your heart one day."

In the midst of worldwide upheaval, I appeared to live a charmed life. I had a devoted husband, two beautiful, healthy children, a lovely home. All around me, young men were going off to war. Brian, though, was safe, working in Military Intelligence in Washington, D.C. I didn't have to worry that he'd be blown apart by enemy bombs overseas. He wouldn't be missing a limb after the war was over. His children recognized him when they saw him because he came home often on leave, even if it was just for a brief twenty-four hours. When peace was restored, we'd resume our tranquil life in Wakefield.

Yet despite everything I had to be grateful for, I couldn't erase Marco from my mind. I knew Carly didn't want to hear that, and I wished I could tell her differently, but the fact is, every time I looked at my son, I was reminded of his biological father. Every time I heard that another boy I'd known at school had died in battle, leaving behind a grieving wife, I was reminded that I, too, had lost someone I loved. Unlike those other women, though, I had to hide my sorrow behind a mask of contentment.

No doubt I was disloyal and undeserving, to be pining for another man when the one I'd married treated me like a queen. And truth to tell, I was weary beyond words of being haunted. Marco was dead everywhere except in my heart. I wished he would die there, too, and leave me in peace.

When the German and Japanese armies surrendered in 1945, I thought my prayers were answered. Although I'd never forget him, I found the pain of remembering Marco had diminished to a bearable ache—the kind, I told myself, inspired by a girl's first love. But at twenty-four I was a woman and smart enough to admit that such youthful, idealistic emotion couldn't have lasted.

Real life was about skinned knees and measles and rained-out picnics. It was visiting the dentist and worrying about diphtheria epidemics and being there for my mother when my father suffered a mild heart attack.

Most of all, it was about being a good wife to my dear husband. If my marriage lacked the tempestuous passion I'd experienced with Marco, it brought me a serenity that filled me with comfort and left me satisfied. Brian and I shared an undemanding love whose strength lay less in sexual gratification than in the quiet pleasure of a couple devoted to each other and their children.

Nothing, I believed, could disrupt the untroubled rhythm of our postwar days. The victory celebrations were over and life was back to normal. In September, Steven entered the kindergarten class at a small private school in the village. We bought a piano and had a teacher visit the house once a week to give him lessons.

Grace got hold of a pair of kitchen scissors one day and cut off a great chunk of her hair. Peggy discovered the evidence at the top of the stairs and for once came to me in tears, instead of the other way around.

"It's my fault," she wept. "I left the blessed things where the child could get them. It's a miracle she didn't scalp herself or poke out an eye."

"It's not the end of the world, Peggy. It'll grow back," I said. But in fact, I was horrified. My daughter was almost bald in front, and we'd planned to give our parents a family portrait for Christmas!

But as it happened, that was the least of my problems. One day in mid-December, I came home after collecting Steven from school to find a blue envelope with a foreign stamp among the Christmas cards in the mailbox. My mother had struck out my old Newport address and forwarded it to me in Wakefield. I recognized her handwriting.

I recognized the original sender's handwriting, too, and the past I was so sure I'd laid to rest rose up to confront me again.

CHAPTER SIX

I'VE REALLY SHOCKED Carly with this latest revelation. She gives a start, almost spilling what's left of her after-dinner coffee, and regards me with wide-eyed horror. "What in the world did you do?"

"I fumbled at the front door, my hands shaking, my stomach churning, and staggered into the house. Peggy, about to go upstairs with clean laundry, stopped dead at the sight of me. 'Whatever is the matter?' she asked me. 'You're pale as a ghost.'"

I recall that I'd echoed her last word. "Ghost?" A high, cracked laugh bounced off the walls, and it had come from me.

Dropping the freshly ironed sheets and pillow slips on the hall tree's storage bench, she rushed forward. "Are you ill, darlin'?"

With an effort, I pulled myself together and helped Steven take off his coat and boots. "Too much running around getting ready for Christmas, Peggy, that's all. I've overdone it, I'm afraid. I might lie down for half an hour this afternoon."

"A very good idea," she declared. "I'll make sure the children don't disturb you."

As soon as lunch was over, I escaped to my room, sank into the chair by the window and slit open the flimsy blue envelope. Three close-written pages spilled out. With trembling fingers, I smoothed the creases from them and started to read.

Back in the present, I show Carly the letter. "Here it is," I tell her, "much the worse for wear, I'm afraid."

Firenze
October 26, 1945
Anna, my dear one,
When I last saw you, I made many promises, very few of which I have kept. A silence of six years hardly entitles me to beg favors of you now, yet I write to you hoping this letter will reach you and that you will not dismiss it, even though you might wish it had never arrived. If nothing else, I need to tell you that it was not by choice that I abandoned you.

You remember from my last correspondence, I am sure, that I held out little hope for my country to escape Mussolini's dictatorship unscathed, but even I did not fully grasp his stranglehold on our right to free speech—until my father was executed. I knew then that I was a marked man. I had a reputation as a dissident, voiced my opinions too freely, associated openly with others of similar mind and my name was Paretti.

I realized that sooner or later, I, also, would be brought to account, and I wrestled with the idea of preparing you for that possibility. But I could no more surrender without a fight the future we both

longed for, than I could turn traitor to my con-
science, so I chose to keep you in ignorance. Eventually I came to regret that decision because it
offered you no explanation for my sudden silence,
but by then, much though I wished I'd done things
differently, it was too late to rectify matters.

Since I obviously did not face the firing squad,
where have I been all these years? you ask. And why
have I waited so long to contact you?

Along with others who shared my political views,
I was imprisoned on Ponza, a remote island in the
Mediterranean, from October 1939 until September 1943, when we were liberated by American
forces. I then joined the Resistance Movement,
fighting the Nazis in the Alps, and later on the Po
plain. While many of my compadres died for our
country, remembering you and hoping the day
would come that we'd be together again gave me the
will to survive.

I finally returned to Firenze this past summer, and
after helping my mother and sisters put their broken
lives together again, set about bringing order to my
own. I returned to a profession I had of necessity ne-
glected for far too long. But even as I worked hard
to refresh my knowledge and add to it, you were
never far from my mind.

At night I walked past the great doors of Santa
Maria Novella and heard the bells ring out the hour. I
stood beneath the window of the room where we spent
our last night together. The memories drew me so
strongly, Anna, that I could smell your perfume. I

heard your voice as clearly as if you stood next to me. I could almost touch you.

I told myself I had no right to contact you. By now, you had surely formed new loyalties, found new love. I should do likewise, and forget you. What, after all, did I have to offer, with my assets seized by the Fascists and my career yet to be established?

But Italy is renewing itself. With skills such as mine in great demand, my prospects have improved. I have been offered a partnership in one of the biggest architectural firms in the city. And try though I might, I cannot forget you, my Anna. You are in my heart forever.

Even when things were at their worst, when death seemed imminent, I was not afraid. But I am afraid now, not of what I might learn, but of what I might never know. Are you well, are you happy, are you alive? These questions hound me and I would give much for them to be answered. But the most pressing question remains to be asked, and I can do nothing other than to state it boldly. Now that our countries are no longer enemies, is there any chance you and I might pick up where we left off and build a future together or is it too late?

I am aware that world events brought about a separation neither of us expected, and that you had no reason to think I would ever come back into your life. Should you choose not to acknowledge this letter, I shall accept it as a sign that you have made a new life for yourself with no room in it for me, and you may be assured I shall not attempt to intrude on it again.

I have loved you for seven years, my Anna. I love you still. Enough to let you go if I must.
Forever yours,
Marco

When I finished reading his letter that December day, I put the letter aside and sat in thought for ages, dazed by my conflicting emotions. Once, I would've given everything I owned to hear from him again. Now, I almost hated him.

"But it wasn't his fault, Gran," Carly surprises me by pointing out.

"That's true. But he'd disappeared from my life without so much as a goodbye. He left me so alone, so adrift, so afraid, that I'd wanted to die. He'd left me pregnant. Without Genevieve and your grandfather, I'm not sure how I would've gone on. Brian, in particular, had carried me through those dark days and brought me to a place of peace and contentment. Now Marco was back, and he'd turned my world upside down again...."

And yet, to hear that he was alive, that he'd never stopped loving me...how could I not rejoice?

But what to do next? I had no answers.

My first instinct was to destroy the letter before it destroyed me and everything I held dear. What purpose would it serve to reopen wounds which had taken years to heal, and imperfectly at that?

To respond could undermine the very foundation of my marriage. In taking me as his wife, Brian had done more than save my reputation. He'd cared for me enough to put my needs before his own. He'd filled me with hope for the future when I was convinced there was none to be had.

Together we'd created a beautiful daughter. He'd accepted Steven as his true son and had never once shown partiality for his own flesh and blood. All good reasons to burn the letter and spare my family the turmoil of letting my first love back into my life.

Downstairs, I heard the thud of the front door closing, and the children's voices rising above a man's deeper tones. Startled, I noticed that dusk had fallen and Brian was home. I barely had time to stuff the letter under a cushion before he came into the bedroom.

Lifting my face for his kiss, I said, "I wasn't expecting you until much later. Weren't you supposed to have drinks at the faculty club after class?"

"I changed my mind," he said.

"Why?"

"Peggy phoned. She thought I should come home."

Annoyed, I exclaimed, "Oh, she shouldn't have done that!"

"She was worried about you, Anna. You weren't yourself when you came back from picking up Steven at school this morning, and you've been shut in here by yourself all afternoon, refusing to let Peggy bring you tea, refusing to speak to anyone." He perched on the stool at my feet and chafed my hands in his. "What is it, honey? What's happened?"

Too troubled to confront him, I glanced aside.

Very gently he turned me to face him again. "Talk to me, Anna. There's nothing you can't tell me. Whatever it is, trust me to understand."

Honesty was such a big part of our relationship. We might have told little white lies over the years, but we'd never kept the important truths from each other. We'd never harbored secrets that could change the course of our lives.

"I received some disturbing news today," I said, my chin quivering helplessly.

"About?"

"Marco."

"And?"

"He's alive."

Brian grew very still. "Are you sure?"

Pulling my hands free, I showed him the letter. "He sent me this."

"What's to prove it wasn't written years ago and only just found its way here?"

"Because it wasn't, Brian." I thrust it at him. "Here, read it for yourself."

A beat of silence passed before he shook the written pages from the envelope and lowered his eyes. I had no clue what he was thinking as he read. None of the anguish I'd felt showed on his face. Rather, he looked frighteningly impassive.

Finally he laid the envelope and its contents on the floor beside him, looked me in the eye and said, "What are you going to do?"

"I don't know," I replied miserably. "What do you want me to do?"

"It's not my decision to make, but this much I can tell you: I won't stand by and let him take Steven away from me. That boy is as much my son as Grace is my daughter, and he's staying that way, regardless of whose blood runs in his veins. Beyond that, it's up to you how you deal with it."

I sighed. "I wish he'd never written!"

"But he did, and now you'll have to deal with it."

"Don't you even *care* what it might do to our family?" I cried.

"Yes, I care," he shot back, white-faced with anger. "He threatens everything that matters to me. But do I blame him, when I'd have done exactly the same thing were I in his place? No, I do not."

"So what are you saying? That I should reply to his letter and invite him into our lives?"

"That's for you to decide."

"Not true, Brian. We have to decide together."

He regarded me with troubled eyes. "Do you still care for him, Anna?"

He'd asked the one question I dreaded. "Yes," I admitted in a low voice, because no matter how it pained me or my husband, this was one of those big, important truths that couldn't be dismissed with a little white lie. "I will always care for him. But not enough to sacrifice what I have with you."

"But enough to tell him he has a son?"

I stared at him, aghast. "Why would I do that?"

"Because," he said wearily, "perhaps he has the right to be told. He didn't abandon you by choice. He spent four years in exile for his ideals, then another two fighting for them. He put his life on the line not just for his country, but for the liberty we all enjoy. Does he now deserve being denied the knowledge that he fathered a son?"

"I hadn't considered that," I faltered. "But, Brian, what if he insists on meeting Steven? What would it do to our son, to discover you're not really his father?"

"Either you must set boundaries, or I will. If Marco loves you as much as he says he does, he'll respect them."

"And if he doesn't?"

"If you have doubts, then perhaps you should think twice before acknowledging his letter. The question then becomes, can you live with yourself, knowing you're deceiving him when he's been honest with you?"

Frustrated, I said, "Sometimes I wish I'd never heard the word 'honest.' I wish I could lie and not feel ashamed."

"You'd never be able to live with yourself," my husband said, his smile tinged with bitterness. "Listen, don't make up your mind tonight. Sleep on it and see how you feel in the morning. Meanwhile, wash your face, put on that pretty red dress and come downstairs. The children have been busy and are excited for you to see what they've made."

Gingerbread men, I discovered, haphazardly decorated with bits of chopped peel, sugar sprinkles and blobs of frosting. "This one's yours, Mommy," Grace crowed, pointing to a cookie dripping with a road map of white icing.

"And I made one for my daddy," Steven said.

His daddy, his hero!

I looked at my two beautiful children. At Grace, a sweet little dumpling, turned four a month ago. At Steven, tall for his age, with the baby fat already melting away, and so handsome that people stopped me in the street to comment. How proud of him Marco would be.

I looked at Brian, saw the understanding in his eyes and made my decision. The next afternoon, he and the children went shopping for a Christmas tree, and I was free to tackle what I knew would not be an easy task.

Wakefield, Rhode Island
Saturday, December 20, 1945
Dear Marco,

I received your letter yesterday and am still so shocked to hear from you that I scarcely know how to respond. I am, of course, overjoyed to learn you're alive, but confess I find it unsettling, too. The past has come back to haunt me in ways you can't even imagine.

Where do I begin to explain what I mean by that? I suppose by telling you everything. I am indeed alive, well and happy and, as you surmised, married. Brian and I grew up next door to each other. He and Genevieve were my salvation during the last weeks of 1939 when I believed I'd lost you.

You remember Genevieve, I'm sure. She's godmother to my children and still my best friend after Brian. She's flirted with love since we were in Italy, but has finally met the man of her dreams and is planning a spring wedding. I'll be her matron of honor. Grace, my daughter, is to be a flower girl, and my son, Steven, the ring bearer.

We live in a village a few miles from Kingston, where Brian teaches at the state college. He enjoys gardening, golf and sailing, and I like baking and sewing for the children.

I'm rambling on about matters that probably aren't of much interest to you, because I'm putting off the most difficult part of this letter. If, in writing to me, you were afraid of what you might learn, believe me when I say I'm much more afraid of what I must tell you. But Brian and I have discussed this at some length and both agree you should know the truth.

The thing is, Marco, although I have two children, Brian fathered only one, our daughter Grace. Although I didn't realize it until much later, Steven was conceived when I was in Italy and is your biological son. Since I can well imagine what a blow this is to you, I don't have to tell you that it struck me equally hard, coming as it did after I had every reason to believe you were dead. To be pregnant and unmarried, and to have lost the love of my life, overwhelmed me.

Grief and shame do not mix well, Marco, and I dread to think what I might have done if it hadn't been for Brian and Genevieve. They risked their own good names in order to preserve mine, proving their love and friendship for me over and over. My pregnancy was confirmed in mid-October and Brian married me within a month. Steven was born seven months later.

Until now, only three people—Brian, Genevieve and I—knew the truth of his paternity. I'm sharing it with you because Brian and I feel you deserve to be told. How you receive this news is up to you. You might prefer to ignore it, or even disbelieve it, and choose not to contact me again. Certainly, making a fresh start will be easier that way. But if you decide you want some involvement in Steven's life, I must make it clear now that you'll play a peripheral role only. To all intents and purposes, Brian is his father, and I beg you in the name of the love we once shared not to compromise that. Occasional news and photographs must be the extent of your association with him. Brian and I have built a happy family out of heartbreak and sacrifice. We won't jeopardize it because fate chose to play a cruel trick on all of us.

I'm aware that this letter will shock you every bit as much as yours shocked me, and I'm sorry for that. But some good things do come out of tragedy. You and I are both alive and doing well, and even though our futures no longer coincide, we will always have a connection through our son. I hope this will be of some comfort to you.

Fondly,

Anna

It took three hours before I laid down my pen, my many false starts crumpled around my feet, but with the final copy done at last. Leaving my writing desk, I stretched and went to stand at the window.

Once again, the afternoon had slipped by without my being aware. The sky to the west had turned a radiant pink. Snow etched the bare limbs of the oaks and maples in the garden, and lay thick on the shrubs Brian had planted. Not a breath of wind stirred the air.

The downstairs rooms smelled of freshly cut fir and cloves. Joining Peggy in the kitchen, I discovered that she'd been busy baking mince tarts. Down the hall, I could hear the children's excited chatter as they helped Brian sort through the Christmas decorations he'd brought down from the attic.

Glad to spend an hour with my family, of whom I'd seen

precious little in the past twenty-four hours, I went to the parlor and walked in on a scene that could've been taken directly from Currier & Ives. Logs blazed in the fireplace. They, and the lamps on the piano and a side table, filled the room with golden light. Framed by the windows, the tree stood tall, untrimmed except for the fistfuls of tinsel the children had flung at its lower branches. Brian knelt on the floor, checking the strings of Christmas lights. Replacement bulbs hadn't been available during the war and were still in short supply.

At first unnoticed, I stood in the doorway, my attention mostly on Steven. With every passing year, he resembled Marco more. People had begun commenting on his appearance, wondering where he came by his black hair and olive skin. "He could be from foreign parts if it weren't for his blue eyes," one of the other mothers at the school had remarked the week before. "Is your husband's family dark?"

"His grandfather was Welsh," I equivocated, relieved that Gavin Wexley had conveniently died many years ago and couldn't be held to account.

Glancing up from his task, Brian saw me on the threshold and raised his brows in silent question. *Is it done?*

I answered with a nod. Seeing me, the children raced across the room and dragged me forward to admire their decorating efforts. We worked together, adding more tinsel, until Peggy came and took them off for their supper.

I'd already changed for dinner, and while they ate, Brian went upstairs to wash away the afternoon's activities and put on clean clothes. "How was it?" he asked, rejoining me in the parlor and pouring us each a glass of sherry.

"Difficult. I left it out for you to see."

"Yes, I saw, but it's between you and Marco, Anna."

"But you and I have no secrets, Brian, and I wish you'd read it to make sure I've spelled out everything that needs to be said."

It, we kept saying, as if by doing so, we could reduce both the letter and Marco to equal insignificance.

"I will, if that'll make you feel better, but I'm confident you've covered everything. The bigger question is, will he keep his distance and be satisfied with the limitations you've set?"

"He'd better be," I said, "because the occasional letter is all he's going to get from me—assuming, of course, that he's even interested in news of the child he fathered."

CHAPTER SEVEN

"OBVIOUSLY, he was," Carly says.

"Very much so, yes."

"I never expected I'd say this, Gran, but I'm beginning to feel sorry for him. I feel sorry for you, too. Reliving all of this isn't easy, is it?"

"No," I admit. "They were difficult days."

"How long before you heard from him again?"

"Quite some time. Airmail wasn't common back then, and surface mail between America and Europe took weeks to cross the Atlantic."

"The waiting must've been hard."

"Not really. With Christmas over, the next big event was Genevieve's wedding, so although I can't say I forgot about Marco, I did manage to push him out of my thoughts much of the time. Maybe at some level I hoped I'd never hear from him again, because whenever he did cross my mind, I got a heavy, sick sensation in the pit of my stomach."

Then, on February 14 of all days, another of those distinctive blue envelopes landed in our mailbox. If anything, I was even more nervous about reading this second letter. What if he planned to show up on our doorstep and demand paternal rights to his son? My well-guarded secret would become common knowledge, thanks to the legal proceedings that would almost certainly ensue, and the one most likely to be hurt by it was Steven.

In the end, though, I'd worried for nothing.

Firenze
February 2, 1946
Dear Anna,

I am in receipt of your letter and, as you inferred, am both saddened and elated by your news. Saddened because I could not be the one you turned to in your troubles. Saddened that another man has taken the place that I, for so long, hoped would be mine. Yet how much I owe your husband, that he stepped willingly into my shoes and gave my son his name. It remains a debt I can never repay.

My son! Even seeing the words and saying them aloud, I am unable to come to grips fully with what they mean. How is it possible, I wonder, that a child of mine was born and I had no inkling of it? We knew such closeness, you and I, that even when we were apart, we often sensed what the other was thinking. Yet when you needed me the most, telepathy failed us. Perhaps it's better that it did because, had I known I'd left you pregnant and been helpless to come to you, I believe I would have gone mad.

None of this, however, lessens my joy at learning I have a son. We have lost so much in Italy. We have been disgraced on the world stage, our national pride is in tatters, our economy in disarray. My mother is left a widow, my sisters and I have lost a father. Yet for me, suddenly, comes the gift of a son, a permanent reminder of the love we shared, Anna, and how can I not rejoice at that?

Where, then, does all this leave us? Our lives follow different paths now, yet there exists between us a bond that can never be broken. Perhaps I am selfish to wish I could become a more tangible part of Steven's life, that he could know me as his father. To teach him about his heritage, show him the city where he was conceived, and introduce him to his grandmother and aunts, would mean so much.

Accepting that this will never be does not come easily, but I take comfort in the fact that you are willing to share him with me, albeit from a distance. So put to rest those fears I detect in your letter, *cara mia*. Although, like you, my son will forever hold a piece of my heart, I shall not trespass beyond the limits you impose. For years now, I have learned to live on dreams and let them sustain me. With your help, I shall continue to do so. Letters from you and, if possible, photographs of my boy, will bridge the distance between us and enable me to achieve acceptance of a situation I am powerless to change.

Thank you, Anna, for trusting me with the knowledge of our child. I am fully aware that, had you chosen to remain silent about him, I would have been none the wiser. Despite my disappointment at the hand I have been dealt, knowing that he has you for his mother and that he is well-loved brings me a measure of peace that has long eluded me.

I wish you and your husband every good thing and hope to hear from you soon.

With deepest affection,

Marco

And so began a regular correspondence between us, which, for a while, seemed harmless. Apart from Brian, no one knew of this latest turn of events, not even Genevieve.

Or at least not until April, when she and I went for the final fitting of our dresses for the wedding. Afterward, we stopped for lunch at the yacht club, and that was when I brought her up to date on my news. By then, Marco and I had exchanged two more letters each.

Her first reaction was one of disbelief, closely followed by horror. "You're doing *what?*" she exclaimed, then, seeing that her outburst had attracted the attention of other guests, lowered her voice to a near whisper and continued, "Tell me I didn't hear you right and that you didn't say you're carrying on with Marco Paretti, long distance."

I glared at her, surprised and more than a little offended. "We're not *carrying on!* We're exchanging civilized letters. Anyway, I was under the impression that you liked him and you'd be glad he's alive."

"Well, it's not that I particularly want to see him six feet under, Anna," she said, "but don't you think you're taking an awful chance by giving him free entry to your life like this?"

"No, because it's different between us now. We're friends, not lovers."

"That doesn't change the fact that he's Steven's real father."

"He's reconciled to that remaining a secret."

"Until when?" Genevieve scoffed. "Because, trust me, sooner or later, he'll try to stake a claim. It's the nature of the beast to want to brag to the whole world that he's got what it takes to sire an heir. And," she finished darkly, "he's Italian. Family's a very big deal with them."

"You're wrong, Genevieve," I insisted. "Marco won't go back on his word."

"Can you guarantee that? It's not as if he's got any other children to occupy his affections."

"Because he's too busy rebuilding his career for marriage to enter the picture."

"Or because he's still carrying a torch for you."

"Well, if he is," I said, "he's wasting his time. I already have a husband."

"Speaking of whom," she said, "is Brian in on all this?"

"Of course he is. We don't keep secrets from each other."

"And he's okay with it?"

"He's…accepted it."

She shook her head, mystified. "Then he's a saint is all I can say, because it's more than Francis would put up with. He'd flatten any former boyfriend of mine who tried to put the moves on me."

"Right now, maybe, but when you've been married as many years as we have—"

"That's got nothing to do with it. When an old flame re-appears on the scene, you become vulnerable."

"Not me," I said smugly. "I'm happy with what I've got."

HER WEDDING, a splashy affair, took place the second Saturday in May, with the ceremony at Trinity Church in Newport, and a reception in the lavish oceanview home of one of the groom's friends. Genevieve was exquisite as she walked down the aisle on her father's arm. Uncle James had never looked prouder as he handed her over to her groom.

Thirty-one year-old Francis Kimball-Jones was probably the most eligible bachelor in Newport. Successful, ambitious and from old money, he'd broken more than a few hearts and there was no question that he and Genevieve made an arresting couple. To me, though, my children were the real stars of the show. Grace wore an ankle-length crinoline dress with pink satin rosebuds along the hem and neckline, and a matching sash. By then, her hair had grown back and fell in Shirley Temple ringlets around her face.

She captivated everyone in the church when she came tripping down the aisle, all dimpled smiles. Then, catching sight of her father in the second row on the bride's side, broke rank and rushed over to announce, "Look at me, Daddy! I'm pretty."

Black-haired, blue-eyed Steven was even handsomer than usual. Already sporting a spring tan, his skin glowed like polished amber against his white ring-bearer's suit. Pride welled up in me, and as the photographer herded us into position for pictures after the ceremony, I made a mental note to order extra copies to send to Marco.

After the honeymoon, the newlyweds were caught up in the Newport social scene for most of the summer, so although we spoke occasionally by phone, I didn't see Genevieve again until the end of August, when she came to spend the day with me. She was very stylish in her summer dress and hat, but had lost weight.

We sat on the porch and sipped lemonade while I

brought her up to date on our doings. "I sent Marco several wedding photographs, including one of me with the children," I told her.

"Really?" she said listlessly. "Have you heard from him since?"

"Yes. Last week."

"How did he like them?"

"He was immensely grateful, especially for more pictures of Steven, and very complimentary about Grace."

"And what did he have to say about you?"

I see that my memories of you have not kept pace with time, Anna, he'd written. *The lovely young girl with whom I fell in love has grown into a woman of beauty, and my heart aches anew at knowing you will never again be mine.*

"Pretty flowery stuff, if you ask me," Genevieve decided, when I quoted this passage to her. "*My heart aches anew,* indeed! Is he always this stiff and artificial?"

Taken aback by her remark, I sprang to his defense. "Remember English isn't his mother tongue. How smoothly would *your* prose flow if you had to write in Italian?"

She averted her gaze, her mouth pinched, her expression grim. "It's not what a man says, it's what he does. Words are meaningless if they're not backed up with actions."

"Marco's not exactly in a position to take action, though, is he? Words are all he's got."

Another tense silence ensued and glancing at her, I saw her eyes were bright with tears. "What's this really all about, Genevieve?" I asked softly.

She made a superhuman effort to smile. "Nothing. Don't mind me. I'm out of sorts today."

That wasn't like her. Genevieve was the kind of woman

who bent life to her will and refused to let it get her down. "Why? What's wrong?"

Again, I had to wait for an answer and strain to hear it when it came. "I had a miscarriage two weeks ago," she whispered.

"Oh, Genevieve, I'm so sorry! How far—"

"Not quite three months."

Steven and Grace were playing on the swing Brian had hung from the oak tree on the back lawn, and I couldn't begin to imagine how hard it must be for her to see my happy, healthy children; how empty she must feel inside, watching them play.

"I'm very sorry," I said again. Inadequate words, admittedly, but the best I could come up with. "How's Francis taking it?"

"Not well," she replied, her tone oddly brittle. "He's highly inconvenienced."

"Inconvenienced?"

"That's right. I had trouble with the pregnancy from the very first—cramping, spotting, that sort of thing. We had to cancel more than one social engagement, and if that wasn't bad enough, we haven't been able to have..." She looked away again, her lips pressed tight.

"Marital relations?" I prompted.

"Sex, Anna," she said flatly, spinning back to face me again. "Francis has been deprived of sex—at least with me."

I stared at her, thunderstruck. "You surely aren't suggesting he's been unfaithful?"

Wrestling her emotions under control, she shrugged. "I really couldn't tell you. I've seen so little of him this past month, I have no idea what he's been doing." Then her composure slipped again, her lips quivering. "He didn't even know I'd lost the baby until three days after it happened."

Once again, I was shocked almost speechless. "You mean, he hasn't been coming home at all?"

"Let's say a number of business trips have arisen lately and necessitated his going to Boston. Overnight."

"They could've been real, darling."

She regarded me tearfully. "Real or not isn't the issue. Would Brian go out of town if you were in danger of losing a baby?"

No, he would not. Struggling to offer her some kind of solace, I said, "A lot of men aren't comfortable being around illness, especially with women. Some can't stand to see their wives in labor. Maybe Francis is one of them."

Her smile broke my heart. "It'd be nice to think so."

She left soon after. Hating to see her go, I walked her around to the front of the house, where her driver waited. At the last minute, she grabbed me in a fierce hug. "You're so lucky, Anna. Brian might not have been your first choice as a husband, but look how your marriage has turned out."

"It's about as solid as it gets," I agreed. "We've had our share of rough patches, the same as everyone else, but we survived and you will, too. You'll see."

"I hope so," she said in a quavering voice, "because I really do love Francis."

"I'm sure he loves you, too."

I prayed that was so, and they were just going through the growing pains that so often came after the honeymoon phase. But what did I know? Brian and I hadn't started out dewy-eyed, so we'd never suffered any letdown when the romantic glow wore off. We'd built our marriage on a foundation of necessity, and a friendship that went back to our childhood. Yes, we loved each other, but we'd never pretended to be *in* love.

Genevieve climbed into the backseat of the car and rolled down the window. "I'll call you next week," she promised. Then, as an afterthought, she said, "Be careful with Marco, sweetie. Don't let him get too close."

I laughed at the very idea. "Not a chance. I'll always be fond of him, but that's the extent of it."

SEVERAL TIMES over the next few months, Genevieve made plans to visit, then called it off at the last minute. Suddenly, the leaves were turning color, Thanksgiving lay just around the corner and the year was fast slipping away. We invited everyone to our house for Christmas dinner, including Aunt Patricia, Uncle James and, of course, Genevieve and Francis. Late on December 24, she phoned to cancel. Francis had been in a car accident and broken his arm.

Her parents were disappointed but resigned when they arrived the next day and heard the news. "Something always seems to come up at the last minute," my aunt complained. "We hardly see Genevieve anymore. You'd think we lived on the other side of the country instead of half an hour's drive away. It's as if we're not good enough for her now that she's married to a Kimball-Jones."

The men exchanged a telling glance. "Or it's the other way around, and Francis isn't good enough for us," my uncle said, but quietly so my aunt didn't hear.

Later, while the men enjoyed an after-dinner cigar and Aunt Patricia was reading to the children, I cornered my mother. "What did Uncle James mean with that remark about Francis?"

"Oh, dear!" she sighed. "I'm afraid Genevieve's marriage might be in trouble. The gossip wouldn't reach you here, of course, but it's common knowledge in Newport circles that Francis is…well, a little wild."

"And Aunt Patricia doesn't have a clue?"

"Not so far. James is doing his best to shield her, but sooner or later she's bound to hear of it and she'll be crushed when she does." Mother drew me into a quick hug. "I'm so grateful and proud you made a better choice, Anna. The best, in fact. Brian would no more dream of being unfaithful to you than you would to him. He's a wonderful husband."

"Yes, he is," I said, knowing she couldn't begin to guess exactly how wonderful. "You'll never have to worry about us, Mother. No one and nothing will ever come between us."

I pause and Carly watches me, her face alive with curiosity. "Did you really believe that, Gran?"

"I really did, precious, because I forgot that we all have our vulnerabilities. It was an easy mistake to make back then. Life in America was very comfortable. The stringent measures of the war years gave way to a more glamorous era. New cars were beginning to roll off the assembly lines. Brian traded in his 1938 Chevrolet for a wood-sided Ford station wagon and taught me how to drive." I smile at the memory.

Femininity was in vogue again. Women wore pretty clothes, and threw out the military styles they'd put up with for so many years. Brian and I caved in to the children's pleas for a pet and brought home a nine-week-old kitten we named Tuxedo because he was all black, except for his white chest and stomach, and magnificent white whiskers. In other words, we fit the demographics of an upscale, postwar American family.

Although Marco and I continued to correspond, it was, I thought, mostly because of Steven. The angst of 1939 had faded, and I convinced myself we wouldn't have had much to say to each other had it not been for our son.

In other words, I grew too complacent. Until the day before Steven's seventh birthday, when the mailman dropped off another letter. I was alone in the house at the time and poured myself a glass of sun tea, then went out to the back porch and sat on the swing to read what was a much shorter message than usual.

May 26, 1947
Dear Anna,
Thank you for your last letter. As always, your news lessens the miles between us and makes me feel closer to Steven. I shall be thinking of him on June 12, and wishing I could share in his birthday celebrations. From his latest photograph, I see he has grown tall, and wonder if he shows a more marked resemblance to me now—or is that merely wishful thinking on my part?

I, too, have undergone some changes since last I wrote. My old friend Rudolfo and I have started our own company and already have won several commissions. As a result, we have hired two more architects and four more draftsmen to ease our workload.

I have bought an apartment in a former palazzo near the Ponte Vecchio. It is considerably larger than my current residence, but in a sad state of disrepair. However, I look forward to restoring it to its former grandeur, along with enough modern touches to please my wife, Giulia Maldini, whom I married last month. Her parents are friends of my mother's—

Despite my best efforts, I couldn't get past this last piece of news. My eyes remained fixed on those two lines and the information he'd dropped so casually into his update—almost as an afterthought—but it slammed into my solar plexus with the force of an iron fist.

Marco married to someone else?

My first shameful reaction was, *He can't be! He's mine!* Several minutes passed before the reality hit home that, in fact, he now belonged to another woman. Then it was as if a floodgate opened and memories I truly thought I'd long since put to rest swept over me.

His image which, over time, had blurred around the edges, grew sharp in my mind, as though I'd seen him as recently as yesterday. The cleft in his chin, the way his dark hair curled against the back of his neck, his smile, the way his gaze used to slide over me, intimate as a kiss, even the shape of his hands, all came back to me with stunning clarity....

I missed him as acutely as I'd missed him almost eight years ago, so ferociously that a howl of pain welled up within me. Although I managed to smother it, I couldn't stem the tears rolling down my face.

Eventually my catharsis passed. Drained, I left the porch, went upstairs and washed my face before finishing what was left of his letter.

I hope this finds you well and happy, Anna. As always, Steven is in my thoughts and in my heart. If wishing were enough to make it so, he would know nothing but happiness and success in the coming year.
Marco

In the calm aftermath of a storm I'd never seen coming, two things occurred to me. First, I was not nearly as "over" Marco as I'd fooled myself into believing. And second, I took comfort in his stark delivery of the news that he'd married, which suggested the decision had little to do with overwhelming passion for the woman who was now his wife, and a great deal more with living up to the expectations of his society.

My assessment was not far off the mark. The next year, his daughter, Claudia, was born and although he gladly embraced everything to do with fatherhood, he made no secret of his disenchantment with his marriage.

Second-best love, he wrote, *is like tepid, overcooked pasta. Unpalatable at best, and sometimes downright intolerable. You created an emptiness in my life, Anna. Accepting that there could be no future for me with you and our son, I tried to fill the void by starting a family that was completely my own. Beyond devotion to my daughter, however, I find no satisfaction in the arrangement. A warm body in my bed at night does nothing to erase my longing for you, the only woman I shall ever love. If, somehow, we could be together, I would move heaven and earth to make it happen. Like yours, my marriage had more to do with convention than substance.*

Reprehensible though it was, I admitted to a sneaking

satisfaction at knowing Marco languished for me from a safe distance. But the difference between us was that I wasn't actively unhappy with Brian. We led a very comfortable life, had many things in common, and we did love each other in a steady, undemanding fashion. If our relationship lacked excitement, it caused me no misery either, and I would do nothing to jeopardize it.

Whether or not my mother would still be proud of me if she could read my mind and discover all my secrets was another matter entirely.

CHAPTER EIGHT

CARLY LOOKS DUBIOUS. "So you were both leading a double life. Didn't his wife ever ask about all those letters from America?"

"She never knew about them. From the first, I'd always sent them to his office."

"But then something changed that upset your routine, didn't it? One look at your face tells me that."

"You're right, darling. One bright afternoon in June, 1950, right after Steven turned ten and school was out for the summer, I was in the garden, weeding a flower bed..."

A shadow fell between me and the sun, and glancing up, I saw Brian. Lately he hadn't been getting home much before seven, and sometimes missed dinner altogether, because in addition to his teaching load, he was researching yet another in a series of papers he was writing for various academic journals.

"You're home awfully early," I said. "Is everything all right?"

"That depends." He helped me to my feet and brushed a kiss over my cheek. "Can the garden wait until later? I'd like to run an idea past you."

"Okay." I headed for the back porch.

He stopped me with a hand on my arm. "Not here. I don't want the children interrupting us."

Curious and even a little apprehensive, I nodded and followed him to the creek that ran through the back of our property. Willow trees lined the bank, the tips of their branches hanging low in the water. Dusting off a bench he'd placed there a few summers back, Brian waited until I sat down, then said, "How would feel about living overseas for a couple of years?"

I blinked. "Where overseas?"

"England."

"I'm not sure," I said slowly. "I've never really thought about it. Why do you ask?"

"I've been offered the chance to work at Cambridge. That paper I wrote last November came to the attention of the head of the math department—full name, Department of Pure Mathematics and Mathematical Statistics."

"My goodness, that's quite a mouthful."

"Isn't it, though! My research is finally paying off."

He was referring, of course, to his list of published credits. They, and not intellectual brilliance or teaching expertise, were what ensured prestige in the academic world.

"Well, it's long overdue," I said. "You've worked hard to earn some recognition. What does this man want you to do?"

"Start on my doctorate with him as my advisor and do some teaching on the side. A working scholarship, if you like."

"My goodness," I said again. "Congratulations! Aren't you flattered?"

"Sure. It's a great opportunity and there's no doubt it

would land me on the top rung of the ladder here when we come back."

"In other words, what you're really saying is you can't afford to turn it down."

"Well, there are other issues to consider before we make a decision, the most obvious being the disruption to the children's lives. They'd be flung into a different school system, have to establish new friends. They'd also—"

"They'll adapt, Brian. Children always do," I interrupted, warming to the idea. "Because of the war, they've never had the chance to travel the way we did when we were their age. It'll do them good to see how other people live."

"What about you, Anna?" he asked soberly. "Can you see yourself scaling down your standard of living? Because travel isn't all that's been affected by the war. England's still dealing with the aftereffects, and they're pretty severe. Many foods are still rationed and housing's at a premium. Cambridge escaped the worst of the bombing, but whatever accommodation we end up with won't be on par with what we've got here."

Across the lawn, my pretty Victorian house dozed peacefully in the sun and I felt a moment's doubt. We'd put down deep roots there. We might have started out on shaky ground as a couple, but we'd ended up building a marriage, a family. Living somewhere else temporarily I could manage, but if we didn't have this place to come back to…

"Would we have to sell the house?" Then, having opened a Pandora's box of problems, I went on. "And what about your position here at the college? Would they hold it for you until we're back? And Peggy? We can't put her out in the cold. She's become part of the family and—"

"Well, that's the other half of the deal," Brian said, stopping me in midflow. "The offer's contingent on our agreeing to an exchange with one of the Cambridge lecturers. What it basically comes down to is this—he and I trade homes and jobs, so all we have to do is pack up our personal effects and leave the rest. The family we'd be dealing with has three small children and they want to keep Peggy on, if she's agreeable. Or she can come with us, if she'd prefer. At the end of the two years, both families go back to where they came from and pick up where they left off—except in my case, I'm hoping for a promotion and a hefty increase in salary."

I digested all this, picturing strangers making themselves at home in our house, and not particularly liking the idea. On the other hand, I recognized what an opportunity this was for Brian. He deserved more recognition for his work and I sometimes felt that, because he was younger than the rest of the faculty, he was taken too much for granted at the college.

"If this is going to further your career, and it's pretty obvious it will, then you don't have much choice but to accept," I said.

He inched closer to me on the bench and hooked an arm around my shoulders. "It's not just about me and my career, Anna," he told me soberly. "You and I need a change—something to make us sit up and appreciate each other a bit more than we do. We've fallen into a rut, a very comfortable rut, I grant you, but…"

I knew what he meant and felt a twinge of guilt. Little by little, our relationship had changed. For over a year now, we'd lived more like brother and sister than husband and wife, and I'd done nothing to change that because

Brian had seemed happy. Now I wondered if he wasn't quite as content as he seemed. He was, after all, a man, with a man's needs.

Taking my silence for hesitation, he went on, "We don't have to decide anything right away. I only got word this afternoon that the proposal's received the go-ahead at both ends, but I have until Monday to give my answer."

"If you accept, when would we have to leave?"

"They'd like me there by the beginning of September."

"That's less than two months away."

He nodded. "It doesn't give us a lot of time." He squeezed my hand. "I just want to say one more thing, then I'll drop the subject for now. My career is important to me, but it doesn't come before you or the children. Either the entire family's in agreement or we forget the whole idea and carry on as we are."

As always, he was willing to put us first and himself last, yet I sensed this was something he really wanted. In fact, he seemed almost desperate for me to go along with it. He asked so little and gave so much that I buried my reservations and said, "No. It really is a wonderful opportunity for all of us. You've earned this chance to get ahead and I won't let you walk away from it."

I saw the relief wash over his face, the smile he couldn't contain, and realized it had been years since I'd seen him this happy. Being on the low end of the totem pole in the college hierarchy must have troubled him more than he'd admitted. "Okay then! So when do we break the news to the children and Peggy?"

"Right away, I suppose, since we'll have to begin making preparations almost immediately."

We talked awhile longer, discussing the pros and cons of such a major change. The pros, we concluded, definitely outweighed the cons.

That night after dinner, we sat everyone down and told them what had happened. Brian explained that we weren't leaving forever, that our home would still be here when we came back, and showed the children where England was on the big globe in the library.

Steven was excited at the prospect, but Grace seemed worried. "Can we take Tuxedo?"

Brian and I exchanged glances. We'd anticipated this question and didn't enjoy having to answer it. Tuxedo had grown into a big, handsome cat and was a very important part of our family. Friendly and affectionate, especially with Grace, he was also one of the best mousers in the state—and to my horror, always willing to share the spoils of his hunting.

"I'm afraid not, sweetheart," her father said. "He'll be much better off if he stays here."

Grace's lower lip trembled. "No, he won't! He'll be lonely by himself. Who'll take care of him?"

Peggy, bless her heart, saved the day. "I will," she said, lifting Grace onto her lap. "I'll feed him lots of fish and milk and let him sleep in my room while you're gone. And we'll both be waiting for you when you come home."

"You don't want to make the trip with us?" I asked her in an aside.

"No, darlin', though I do thank you for asking. But I like to be close by my boys and their families. I'll stay here and see to it that those English don't take liberties with your house."

The next few weeks were filled with preparations and saying goodbye to our relatives. On August 18, I once again boarded the *Queen Mary* and set sail for England with my husband and children.

Genevieve was living in New York by then and came to see us off. Finally having had enough of the unfaithful, alcoholic Francis Kimball-Jones, she'd divorced him two years earlier and was now married to Charles Harrison, a widowed financier twenty years her senior.

"Be careful," she murmured, enfolding me in a last hug. "You'll be a lot closer to Italy over there than you are here, and we both know what *that* could mean."

She was referring, of course, to my ongoing contact with Marco. But he and I had established a satisfying long-distance relationship, and I saw no reason for that to change. There'd still be several countries and a considerable body of water separating us. "Not all that close," I whispered back. "In any case, I'm going to have my hands full being a faculty wife and a mother. I won't be crossing the Channel on this trip."

Settling my family in England was a lengthy business, and it was nearly three months before I finally wrote to Marco again.

Cambridge, England
November 18, 1950
Dear Marco,
I'm sorry I haven't written sooner, but as I mentioned in my last letter, Brian accepted the offer from the university here and that allowed little time for anything but preparing for the move. In theory, it

was supposed to be easy, since we brought only our personal possessions. But that, we found out, covered such a wide range that many things dear to us had to remain behind.

This was especially hard on the children and me. Our lives have always revolved around our home and the memories it holds. When it came right down to it, we couldn't simply walk away and abandon it to strangers who might not recognize its importance to us. So although the essentials stayed in place, things we particularly treasured had to be crated and stored elsewhere.

We came by sea, crossing the Atlantic on the *Queen Mary,* and I confess it brought back many memories of when I walked her decks in 1939. I cried myself to sleep every night on that other voyage, so unhappy at having to leave you, and so afraid for your safety. It's as well I had no idea that the worst was yet to come, or I doubt I could have gone on. Yet what I learned from that terrible period is that miracles do happen. You and our son are living proof of that.

Speaking of Steven, you'll be glad to hear that he's adapted extremely well to the English way of life. Already he talks about going to "the pictures" instead of the movies, and has developed a taste for fish and chips served in a folded section of newspaper. At school, he plays football, which is nothing like American football. At home, he was in Grade 5. Here he's in Form 4, the last year of elementary school, and in the spring will take the Eleven Plus exam to determine which secondary school he'll attend.

Grace has adapted less easily to our new life. She's teased by the children in her class because of her accent, misses Peggy and the cat and clings to me when I drop her at school in the morning. I'm hoping she'll adjust and become happier as she grows more used to the customs here.

Our house is a "semidetached," which in America would be called a duplex, and nicer than I expected. It sits on a quiet, tree-lined road, about twenty minutes from the university. There are roses growing under the bay windows in front, and a long lawn in back, sloping down to the banks of the River Cam, which brings home a little closer as we have something similar in our garden in Wakefield. Before the weather turned so cold, we often watched punters gliding along on sunny days, the women holding parasols to protect their peaches-and-cream complexions and the men in white "flannels"—which is an odd way to us Americans to describe trousers, especially as the same word also means "facecloth" here.

There's also quite a large vegetable patch, a reminder of the wartime Victory gardens. Brian enjoyed it when we first arrived. But he loves the academic scene more, so now spends most of his time at King's College, leaving the house shortly after eight in the morning and often not returning before nine or ten at night.

Despite this, our social calendar is very full. There always seems to be some function or other that we must attend—sherry with the department head, afternoon tea with the dean's wife, cricket matches on

Saturdays back in September, and rugby games now. Sunday is the one day reserved exclusively for the children. We explore the neighboring countryside, going by bus as we don't yet have a car. They drive on the wrong side of the road here, which takes some getting used to, and is probably my biggest worry with the children. I'm forever reminding them to look *right* before they cross. During the Christmas break, we plan to venture farther afield and take them to London for a few days of sightseeing.

So there you have it, Marco, a brief update on my doings, most of which I'm sure you'll find boring. But as you can see, we are all well and I really don't have time to be homesick. I do, though, think of you often and hope to hear from you soon.
As always,
Anna

He replied within the week.

Firenze
November 26, 1950
My dear Anna,
So many weeks passed with no word from you that I had begun to fear you might never write again. You can imagine, therefore, the relief and pleasure I felt when I found your letter waiting at my office this morning. Be assured, *cara,* that I could never find your news boring. On the contrary, it lends meaning to my days and keeps me warm at night.

You speak of the memories that came back to you

during your voyage across the Atlantic. I, too, remember that time, especially the morning I stood helplessly by while your train pulled out of the station here in Firenze. I saw your face at the carriage window. I watched it grow smaller and more distant until you were but a blur. Long after you'd disappeared, I remained there, held fast in a desolation that turned the bright day dim, even though not a cloud marred the sky. You carried more than my child, Anna. You took the light and left me filled with darkness.

I have learned to live with that and to take satisfaction in my professional accomplishments. Rudolfo and I enjoy great harmony in our partnership. My work is increasingly well-received, my reputation favorably established, and I can say in all truth that I have achieved a level of success beyond anything I thought possible when the war ended. Perhaps I am like your Brian in that my work consumes me, often to the exclusion of everything else. It is my salvation.

Is this why a man and woman marry? I often ask myself. So that they can then go in opposite directions and spend as little time as possible nurturing their relationship?

In your case, I suspect not. Your contentment shines through in your letters, and for that I am deeply grateful, both for your sake and our son's. In the photographs you send, he is always smiling and I smile back whenever I look at him. Although our time together was brief, Anna, we created something of lasting beauty in him, and I take great pride in the fact that he is of my blood. Yet he reminds me also of what I have lost, and that fills me with a loneliness I reveal only to you, which is why I share your letters with no one. What you and I had together is ours alone.

You speak of miracles, Anna, and you are mine, never far from my thoughts. As long as you live, so, too, shall I.

Marco

This letter troubled me so greatly, I could hardly begin to answer it. For a start, it was briefer than those he usually sent, which struck me as odd considering it had been months since I'd heard from him. That after such a lengthy silence he said nothing about his wife didn't particularly surprise me because he rarely mentioned her. But Claudia, his daughter, was his joy, and he always wrote about her in great detail. Until now.

Although he didn't say it in so many words, reading between the lines I sensed a deep unhappiness in him. His work appeared to be his refuge, his one source of satisfaction. Also, he'd made open reference to his feelings for me, something he'd seldom done before, apart from his initial letter in 1945. And I responded to it because I, too, was lonely.

After we set up house in Cambridge, Brian displayed an almost obsessive need to be with me—for us to do things together, to be seen together around town, whether it was shopping at the open-air market or strolling along the River Walk. But however good our intentions, we soon slid back into our old habits. Indeed, rather than grow closer, we drifted further apart. Not that we fought or anything like that. We still enjoyed being with the children most weekends. We still showed up at all the right university functions.

"Are you saying it was all an act?" Carly asks forlornly.

"No," I hurry to assure her. "The bond of affection remained very real and very strong. But at a deeper level, we led separate lives. The only way I can describe it is that we were traveling on parallel tracks—in accord, but never quite meeting."

I grew increasingly restless and dissatisfied. I loved my children and wouldn't be without them for the world. But I was more than a mother. I was a woman turning thirty at the end of March—still young, yet I felt more like fifty. People I met in England were more reserved than Americans and tended to be much more formal. For most of the time I lived there, I was "Mrs. Wexley" far more often than I was "Anna."

Although I tried not to let it show, I missed my parents, my in-laws, Peggy and Genevieve. There was an emptiness inside me that nothing managed to fill, and I never felt it more keenly than on Christmas Eve when Brian and I took the children to midnight Mass at King's College Chapel.

I expected the usual carols and was not disappointed. What I had not anticipated was how deeply moved I would be by the sights and sounds surrounding me. The atmosphere was, quite simply, holy. I broke out in goose bumps and had tears running down my face, listening to the voices of those fourteen men and sixteen boys singing "Once in Royal David's City." They began with one soprano soaring to the fan vaulting of that magnificent building until, by the last verse, the whole choir had joined in.

Next to me, Grace yawned and leaned against her father. Steven picked at a loose thread on his scarf. Brian checked his watch and I knew his mind was back at the college, not here with us.

Suddenly I missed Marco desperately. He lived and breathed the history of Florence and its many beautiful buildings. I recalled the passion with which he'd shown me its churches and the Renaissance treasures of the Uffizi, and I wished with all my heart that he was standing next to me now, because he was the only one who'd understand the emotions overwhelming me.

I stop talking, sensing that I've already disillusioned my lovely granddaughter. I can't tell her of the bone-deep ache that spread through me and filled me with regret and longing for the heated urgency between a man and a woman who need each other in order to feel alive. For the insatiable hunger to possess and be possessed by the one person in the world who could make you feel complete and sated. For the urgent, often incoherent words of love that sing in your heart like music.

"A pointless exercise, of course," I finally continue. "There was no turning back the clock. I'd made my choices and would have to live with them."

But it didn't prevent my yearning for the impossible. And that, I knew, was not a good thing.

CHAPTER NINE

MAYBE PART of the reason I became so emotional on Christmas Eve had to do with a food parcel that had arrived from the States earlier in the day. Discovering gifts from my parents—my favorite chocolate and special treats for the children—as well as Peggy's maple fudge, fruit cakes and rum puddings made me aware of just how far away I was from all that was dear and familiar.

"Your first Christmas away from home is hitting you hard, isn't it?" Brian observed the next morning as we cleared up after the children had opened their presents.

I glanced at our tree in the curve of the bay window, its spindly branches already dropping needles. "It's simply not the same here," I said.

"I know." He pulled me into his arms and held me close, something he didn't do as much anymore. Not that we weren't affectionate with each other, but we showed it mostly with a brief hug and kiss in the morning and again at night. "What do you say to our spending a few days in London? We can take the children to a pantomime and do some sightseeing and shopping. We talked about doing that before we came here, remember?"

I remembered. Although only four months had passed

since then, it sometimes seemed more like four years. "I'd like that," I replied, wanting nothing more than to recapture my old sense of contentment and well-being.

For a while, I almost succeeded. London's energy and pageantry revived my flagging spirits. Too soon, though, it was back to reality. Within a week of school's starting, both children came down with chicken pox. Grace fell ill first and passed it on to Steven, who waited until she was nearly recovered before he broke out in spots. A gray, cold January dragged into a colder, grayer February.

In the grip of a malaise I couldn't seem to shake, I watched the icy rain sluicing down the windows and yearned for the bright blue skies of a New England winter. I was sick and tired of having to wear heavy sweaters to stay warm in the house. Of waking up in the morning and diving into my clothes before I froze to death in our chilly bedroom. Of running out of hot water or having the oven turn off before a cake had finished baking because I'd forgotten to stuff more shillings in the gas meter.

I'd had my fill of a conductor seeing me racing to catch a bus, and then banging his stupid bell to alert the driver to move on to the next stop, leaving me stranded a few yards away.

And contrarily, I was frustrated by English politeness, by the stoicism people showed. They were so tough, so resilient, so accepting of substandard living conditions and lousy service. After all they'd gone through, they deserved better.

None of this seemed to affect the others in my family. Brian was again immersed in academia. The children didn't need me as they had when we first got here. They'd formed friendships, made an adjustment that eluded me. I felt hemmed in by the narrowness of English life. I wanted more than "going to the shops" every day, as my neighbors put it—a necessity, I admit, since almost no one had a refrigerator at home—and dropping by the nearest pub on weekends. The novelty had worn off tea parties with graduate wives and evenings of intellectual small talk with department heads. Without my knowing how or when, the serenity I used to take for granted had slipped away when I wasn't looking and left me raw around the edges.

I should have listened to Genevieve. My body might be in England, but my thoughts frequently turned south across the Channel to Italy, and Marco. I lived for his letters, and they never disappointed.

Perhaps if I could've confided in Genevieve, I might have been less susceptible to him. But she and I weren't as close as we used to be. She was busy being the wife of a successful New York financier; not only that, she'd always been a terrible correspondent. Even if she'd written more often, she'd never been one to suffer fools gladly and would have been quick to point out *I told you so!*

I'd have given a lot to spend a day with my mother, except what could I have said to her? That my cousin had been right, that the proximity of Italy pulled me like a magnet, and maintaining a balance between past and present was becoming increasingly difficult? Hearing that would have shattered her belief in me.

Once, I could have talked to Brian, but even when he was home, which was seldom, he was preoccupied. There in body but not in mind. One weekend in March, for example, a brisk, sunny day for a change, he forgot to show up for Steven's soccer match, something he'd always done. "Your game was this morning?" he said, sounding surprised that it was Saturday. "I guess I lost track of the time."

By late spring, I was more than just lonely. I was isolated. Trapped in an eleven-year-old secret and hounded by memories of a more glorious time, one filled with a passion the English didn't seem to understand. So I turned to the only person who would.

Cambridge
May 15, 1951
Dear Marco,
Again, this letter is months overdue, and for that I'm sorry. More than once, I've sat down to write but been unable to finish because there is so much I've wanted to say to you and have been afraid to put into words. Silence, though, is smothering me and does nothing to erase you from my thoughts.

In one of your letters, you questioned why people marry, and you must know why I did. Brian and I never pretended to be madly in love, but we were truly fond of each other and made a rational choice to join forces for Steven's sake. If I had to describe what's held our marriage together, I'd say it's a harmony of spirit. We may not share the same interests, but we have the same values. One of the qualities I admire most in him is his even-handed generosity with our children. No one would ever guess he isn't Steven's biological father. If for no other reason than this, I will love him for the rest of my life.

Lately, though, I've been asking myself this question. What if I'd been braver and dared to bring our child into the world without a wedding ring on my finger? If I'd listened to my heart instead of my head? If I'd had more faith in my parents' love, instead of assuming they'd disown me and my baby?

But hindsight is pointless, and I try to focus on how lucky I've been to find a husband who knew from the outset that he took second place to you in my heart, and who accepted me anyway because he doesn't have an envious or selfish bone in his body—which is a lot more than can be said of me. When you told me you'd taken a wife, my first reaction was that you belonged to *me,* and loving me and Steven from a distance should have been enough. I felt you'd betrayed me by letting another woman into your life. (You see what I mean about being selfish?!)

You don't have to tell me I'm also vain, self-centered, conceited, arrogant and any number of other unpleasant qualities. I soon reached that conclusion and told myself I should be glad that, like me, you'd met someone with whom to share your life. I was sincerely happy for you when Claudia was born and hoped holding your baby daughter in your arms might make up, at least a bit, for all that you missed with Steven.

Now, though, I sense such unhappiness in you that you don't even seem to enjoy your little girl anymore, and this brings me to the main purpose behind this letter.

The plain truth is, I'm spending too much time thinking about you, Marco, and given our history and the special place you hold in my heart, that's a dangerous path to follow. So please tell me I'm mistaken and that your life is too fulfilling for regrets.

I'm enclosing Steven's latest school photograph. He's earning top grades in class, excels at sports, is on the school swim team and is thrilled that we're spending next Christmas in St. Moritz so he can learn to ski. He tells me he wants to be a doctor when he grows up, but that's likely to change, as last month he was determined to join the navy, and before that decided he'd like to be a bricklayer, having spent a morning watching a man build a garden wall down the road from us! Above all, though, he's kind and sensitive and very popular with his schoolmates. Whatever mistakes you and I might have made, we got him exactly right and I'm very proud of him.

Yours,

Anna

The minute I mailed the letter, it dawned on me that in speaking so honestly to Marco, I'd opened a door better left closed. That I was right became clear soon enough. His reply arrived by afternoon post on a beautiful day, with the lilacs in bloom and the sky for once washed clear of cloud.

That morning, we heard that Steven had passed the Eleven Plus exam. All his friends received the same news and an impromptu celebration was planned at a house three doors down from us. I was in the middle of mixing cake batter when Grace came home from school and picked up Marco's letter on the front hall mat. "Who's this from?" she asked, inspecting the envelope closely.

As guilty as if I'd been caught shoplifting, I snatched the

letter out of her hand and shoved it in my apron pocket. "Just someone I met ages ago, before you were born."

"You didn't tell me you had a pen pal."

"Well, it's not a secret, if that's what you're thinking. Your father knows about it."

Overreacting might not have been in Grace's vocabulary, but the expression on her face told me she understood it anyway. "I just wondered if I could have the envelope when you're done with it, Mommy, that's all."

Belatedly I remembered she'd joined the stamp club at school. Feeling foolish, I said, "Oh…sure, honey. Sorry if I snapped at you."

"That's okay." She smiled sunnily and leaned against the kitchen table to watch me work. "What're you making?"

"Lemon cupcakes. Steven and his friends passed the grammar school entrance exam, so we're having a party and you're invited."

"Smashing! Can I lick the bowl when you're finished?"

"As long as you wash your hands first," I said, amused by my little American's very English turn of phrase.

I didn't get a chance to read Marco's letter until after the children were in bed, and right from his opening salutation, I knew my fears were well-founded.

Firenze
May 31, 1951
Dearest Anna,
How do I begin to thank you, not just for the news and photograph of Steven, but that you care about me enough to write as you did, from the heart? We spent but a few short weeks together and have been apart

now for almost twelve years, yet you understand me better than anyone else. Better, perhaps, than I understand myself. What, therefore, is the point in trying to deceive you? There is none, so I will give you the truth you requested.

The reason I married is simple. I hoped that by taking a wife, I might forget you. How foolish! Four years in a prison camp did nothing to dim my memory of you, nor did two years of fighting the Nazis. Why would marriage succeed where they failed? The best it could ever do was paint a poor imitation of what I might have had with you, if fate had not been against us.

Giulia and I were drawn to each other by the common thread of trying to repair the damage our families suffered in the war. Her parents lost their other child, her brother. My mother was a widow and, as you know, I am her only son. Both families looked to us for solace. For Giulia's parents, a grandson who might help fill the empty space in their hearts. For my mother also, a grandson who would carry on the Paretti name.

I never expected to find love such I'd known with you, but I hoped that with Giulia I could achieve what you have created with Brian. When she became pregnant, I believed I had succeeded. A child brings its parents closer, I thought, and for a while, it appeared that I was right. When Claudia was first placed in my arms, I felt full in a way that I had not in a very long while. The persistent ache of wanting you and my son eased and grew more bearable. I was deeply grateful to my wife for bearing another child for me to love, openly and without reservation.

What I did not realize was that Giulia was in many respects still a child herself and that she would remain so. Motherhood did not come easily to her. Indeed, it overwhelmed her. She was afraid of the baby. Often, I'd return to our apartment at the end of the day to learn she was at her parents' home, with her mother looking after both her and our child.

I hoped this dependence would eventually fade, and that as Claudia thrived, Giulia would relax and enjoy her as much as I did. It did not happen. Rather, the situation worsened. Her daily visits to her child-hood home have become frequent overnight stays and she is more firmly attached than ever to her mother's apron strings. Essentially I find myself living as a bachelor. The daughter I fell in love with is closer to her maternal grandparents than she is to me, her father. My own mother seldom sees her.

If I could, I would end the marriage. But divorce is no more an option for me now than bearing an il-legitimate child once was for you. We are prisoners within our societies and the limitations they place on us, Anna. The difference is, you have created within those boundaries a marriage worth preserving. Mine has deteriorated to an empty shell of religious and fi-nancial obligation. I love Claudia very much, but from a distance, as I must love Steven.

You speak of how you would make different choices if you could go back in time. I'm sure I don't have to tell you how I would change history, were it

within my power to do so. As it is, I thank God for my work, for the good health my children enjoy, and for having had you into my life, albeit for too short a time. You are and always will be my one true love.
Marco

That letter was the first of many I kept from Brian because, as I soon realized, the tone of my relationship with Marco had slowly spun full circle from that of friends back to that of former lovers still hopelessly drawn to each other. Memories I'd suppressed filtered to the surface, rendering lukewarm the mild passion that had always defined my marriage. And with Brian spending the greater part of his life at the college, I had plenty of opportunity to indulge them—and to reminisce with Marco.

The red roses under my living room window are in full bloom, I told him in June. *The other day, I brought some into the house and this morning saw that one had dropped its petals on the dining room table. They reminded me of our last night together. Do you remember…?*

I do more than remember, he replied. *Whenever I pass a flower-seller on the street, I think of you and those final hours before we had to say goodbye. Not a day passes,* tesoro, *that something I see or hear or touch doesn't bring you back to me….*

And so it went throughout the summer and into fall. Harmlessly seductive exchanges, I tried to convince myself. Except they weren't harmless at all because they flattened the barriers I'd erected to keep Marco at a distance and, as I learned in November, misled him into assuming the basic rules of our association ceased to apply.

Since we have grown closer, I believe a new trust has sprung up between us, Anna, he wrote. *This encourages me to ask something of you that I hope you will consider objectively and not see as a threat to you, your marriage or your family. I would like to meet my son, not to undermine your husband's role as his father, or disrupt his life at all, but simply to see him for myself, to shake his hand and converse with him....*

How is that possible? I wrote back. *To begin with, the miles between us present an obstacle and surely you don't expect me to bring him to Italy?*

He replied by return mail. *Of course not. I will come to England. We can arrange to meet, by accident as it were, in a public place.*

Rather than trying to fend him off with excuses, I should have issued a flat refusal from the beginning. Instead I'd unintentionally given him reason to think I'd consider his request. Realizing my mistake, I tried to correct it.

What you suggest is out of the question, Marco, and unfair to all of us. I refuse to involve my son in a scheme based on outright deception, and I resent your asking me to do so. You will be disappointed by this, but you agreed to abide by my terms when I told you the truth about Steven, and have managed to live with them for the last six years. Please don't ask me to relax them now because your wife is denying you rightful access to your daughter.

I hoped I sounded firm, rational and in control. In fact, I was terrified—of seeing Marco again, of the emotions he aroused in me and of endangering my marriage. Most of all, I was terrified for my sweet, sensitive eleven-year-old son who'd grown up believing Brian was his father. No secret was ever absolutely safe. How would he deal with the truth, should it ever be revealed?

I wasn't about to risk finding out and was greatly relieved when it seemed that Marco had taken my refusal to heart.

"Unfortunately," I tell Carly, "I was wrong." I didn't allow for the single-minded determination that saw him weather four years of prison camp, and two more fighting the Nazis.

CHAPTER TEN

WIDE-EYED, Carly stares at me. "What did he do?"

"At Christmas he tracked us down in St. Moritz."

"He broke his word?"

"Yes."

She blows out a long breath. "You know, I probably would've done the same thing, in his place."

"You surprise me," I say.

"I surprise myself," she admits ruefully. "But the more I hear, the sorrier I feel for him, alienated from his daughter, and still in love with a woman he can't have. It's a rotten way to live. But don't let me stop you, Gran. I want to hear what happened next before I decide he's really one of the good guys."

"Well, our hotel was charming, a classic chalet with a steep roof, painted eaves, deep-set windows, big open fireplaces where we warmed up with hot chocolate at the end of the day, and food of a quality we hadn't enjoyed since leaving America.

"The weather couldn't have been better, with fresh snow piling up on the hill overnight and blue skies greeting us every morning. After a couple of lessons, the children took to the beginners' hill as if they'd been born on skis. Even your grandpa forgot his work and remembered what it was like to relax and have fun. As holidays went, this came as close to perfect as any I'd ever come across—until two days before we were to return to England, and everything fell apart…."

We were in line at the rope tow when the eerie sense that I was being watched made the hair on the back of my neck stand up. Turning, I scanned the area behind us and locked gazes with a man standing a little apart from the crowd. Even with sunglasses hiding his eyes, I recognized Marco at once and nearly fainted with shock.

Unaware of what had occurred, Brian and the children headed up the slope, assuming I'd be right behind them. Instead I stood paralyzed. All around, people were nudging past me, asking none too politely why I was holding them up and suggesting that, if I didn't want to ski, I should remove myself and make way for those who did.

Stomach churning, I floundered in the snow. Searching for an escape from them, from Marco, I almost fell over my poles. At that point he skied smoothly forward, grabbed me by the arm and pulled me aside. "*Ciao,* Anna," he said.

At his touch and the sound of his voice, the cold fear that had gripped me melted in a burst of anger. "Why are you here?" I asked, flinging off his hand.

A stupid question, of course. We both knew exactly why.

"I couldn't stay away," he said. "I had to see him."

"Why? So you could ruin his life and mine?"

"You know me better than to suggest that, Anna."

"No, I don't," I said, my voice quivering uncontrollably.

He reached out as if he thought I was about to cry, then realizing I was too furious for tears, changed his mind and let his hand fall to his side again. "I wish I could say I'm sorry, but that would be a lie. However, I can tell you in all honesty that I never intended for you to see me here."

"But you made sure I did anyway!"

He shrugged. "No. If that had been my aim, I could have achieved it days ago. I came to St. Moritz before you did and have been observing you almost from the minute you got here."

"Observing?" I sputtered. "Don't you mean *spying?*"

"Call it that if you like."

If I liked? "I don't like!" I raged, incensed by his dispassionate acceptance. "What kind of man abandons his own family at Christmas, in order to wreak havoc on someone else's? What did you hope to gain? Did you think I'd let you take Steven away from me? Or were you hoping I'd leave my husband and daughter and run off with you?"

Neither flinching in the face of my rage nor making any attempt to refute my accusations, he said quietly, "Perhaps you should control yourself, Anna."

"Why? Am I embarrassing you?"

"No, but you are, perhaps, embarrassing yourself. Your children are approaching and clearly wonder why you're berating an apparent stranger."

I drew in a horrified breath and swung around. Sure enough, the children had completed their run down the bunny hill and stood a few feet away. Beside myself, I shouted, "Where's your father, and why aren't you with him? Haven't we told you always to stay with one of us?"

"Well, we did, Mom," Steven said, his eyes moving warily from me to Marco. "We're with you—sort of. And Dad's right behind us."

Indeed he was, skiing in their tracks and coming to a stop in a spray of snow beside me. "We lost you," he said, pushing back his goggles. "What happened?"

"He did," I practically screeched, pointing to Marco. I was still so distraught it didn't occur to me that my children were at a loss to understand why their normally sane mother was acting like a raving lunatic. "Guess who, Brian!"

Taking stock of the situation and reaching all the right conclusions, he took immediate steps to halt matters before they spun completely out of control. "Marco Paretti," he said, his glance veering from Steven to the man I'd promised would never be a threat to our family. "What a concidence running into you here."

Betraying not a speck of discomfort at being caught out, Marco continued the charade. *"Si."* He gave me a smile, although perhaps no one else realized how strained it was. "Anna thought she was seeing a ghost."

"I'll bet she did," my husband replied, a hint of steel underlying his affable tone.

"I apologize if I upset you, Anna. That was not my intention." Boldly, Marco's attention skimmed past me and came to rest on Steven and Grace. "These must be your children, yes?"

Sensing the panic I could barely contain, Brian slung a supportive arm around my shoulders. "That's right. Steven, Grace, say hello to Mr. Paretti."

"Hi," they chorused.

"Ciao," he said, his voice suddenly as thick and hoarse as if he'd swallowed gravel. "I am very happy to meet you at last. And please call me Marco."

Oh, how clever they were, these two men, reassuring my children by practicing a monumental deceit without once uttering an actual lie! I should have been grateful. Instead I hated both of them for being able to do what I could not.

"Is your family with you?" Brian asked.

Visibly struggling to rein in his emotions, Marco shook his head. "No. My wife doesn't care for winter sports and my daughter is too young."

"Then perhaps you'll join us for dinner tonight. We'd like that, wouldn't we, Anna?"

I stared at him as though he'd suddenly begun speaking in foreign tongues. *What?*

"Dinner, honey," Brian repeated steadily. "At our hotel. A chance to catch up on each other's news."

"*Grazie.* I accept with pleasure," Marco said, brazenly cutting me off before I could rescind the invitation.

Numb with terror, I stood there while my husband and my former lover finalized the arrangement and my children stared at this fascinating newcomer with the foreign accent, lean, tanned face and dazzling smile. "You scared us when we heard you shouting. We thought you were mad, Mommy," Grace whispered.

I was, but not for the reason she supposed. I was clinging to sanity by a thread. Brian must be, as well, to have invited the wolf into the fold.

The very second we were alone, I lit into him. "Whatever possessed you to ask him to dinner?"

"I figured it was preferable to pretending he wasn't there."

"Well, you figured wrong!"

He pinned me with his candid blue eyes. "Anna, the cat's out of the bag, and there's no stuffing it back in again," he said, pointing out what was all too obvious. "Now it's up to us to deal with it."

"How? By telling him where we're staying? By welcoming him into our family? How does that help anything?"

"He's already come face-to-face with Steven. For us to assume he'll be satisfied with one brief meeting is both foolish and risky."

My heart skipped a beat. "What are you saying?"

"That for Steven's sake, the wisest thing we can do is minimize the danger and try to arrive at a civilized compromise with the man."

"What sort of compromise?"

"I suspect it'll have to be something along the lines of reasonable but supervised visitation."

"Give him access to our son, you mean?" I asked incredulously. "Not as long as I have breath in my body!"

"It's better than having him go behind our backs to see him. And he will, if you try to prevent him. I would, in his place. Steven's a boy any man would be proud of."

That he was right dismayed me immensely. "I wish we'd never come here," I said miserably. "Now nothing'll ever be the same again."

"No, it won't." He tilted his head, apparently absorbed in the distant snow-covered peaks rising sharp against the deep blue sky. "How did he bump into us? Was it coincidence?"

"No," I confessed, remembering. "I mentioned it in one of my letters, back in the summer."

"I see."

"But I didn't invite him to join us, Brian! Nor did I suspect that he'd take advantage of what I'd told him." I glanced at him. "How did you recognize him? I don't recall ever showing you a photograph."

He smothered a laugh. "Good God, Anna, Steven's the living image of him."

"But *you're* his father, Brian."

A slow, rather sad smile crossed his face. "I've tried to be, but it looks as if I'm going to have to share the honor from now on."

"How can you be so calm about it?"

"Calm?" he echoed bitterly. "I'm not calm, Anna, I'm seething inside. I could kill the man for what he's costing me, but I'd rather die myself than let my son know how deeply I resent his biological father."

But I wouldn't let Brian be the one to pay, I promised myself. That night's dinner would be a one-time occurrence. Marco would *not* insinuate his physical presence into my life or my family's. His marriage might be about to self-destruct, but mine, however imperfect, was still intact.

I came downstairs that evening, sure nothing could undermine my resolve. However, I hadn't allowed for how proximity to him would affect me. Even though I'd recognized him instantly that morning, his sunglasses, knitted toque and bulky jacket had acted as a protective barrier between us, just as our correspondence had its own built-in safety shield. Now, in narrow après-ski pants and a dark red sweater, he was again the man I'd once loved so deeply, all lean, hard muscle and dark good looks.

Brian and the children went to greet him, but I hung back at the foot of the stairs, needing a moment to still the giddy lurch of my pulse. He shook my husband's hand, then my son's, and bent to say something to Grace that made her laugh. Straightening, he stared over the heads of the guests milling about the lobby and speared me with a glance that made me go hot all over.

I reminded myself that he was no longer my lover, possibly not even my friend. That lowering my defenses could bring about repercussions worse than anything I'd imagined when I'd first found myself pregnant and believed that he'd been killed. But my head had never been any sort of match for my heart where he was concerned, and keeping a firm grip on my determination was like trying to hold water between my fingers. It leaked away, and left me with nothing to fight him.

Praying my lack of composure didn't show, I joined the group. "Well," I said dully, "here we are. Have we kept you waiting?"

"Half a lifetime it seems," he replied, his dark sweeping appraisal taking in everything about me, from the hem of my long black velvet skirt to the heightened color I knew stained my face. "But it's been worth it. Thank you again for asking me to be with you tonight."

Save your continental charms for someone else, I felt like telling him as we trooped into the dining room and were shown to a table near the fireplace. *They're wasted on me.*

I very deliberately seated Steven between me and Brian, and put Grace on my other side. "We should order quickly," I said. "The children have had a busy day and I'd like them in bed early, since tomorrow's our last day and we want to make the most of it."

"And then it's back to England, yes?" Marco focused all his attention on the children. "Tell me what you like best about living there."

Very clever, Marco, I thought resentfully, as their initial shyness evaporated in the warmth of his smile and they tried to outdo each other with their opinions. Yet to be fair, he divided his attention equally between them and I could point to nothing in his manner or his questions to justify my hostility.

"What is this 'smashing' you speak of?" he teased, after they'd regaled him with a boisterous account of their visit to Madame Tussauds when we were in London. "Surely such well-mannered young people did not attack one of the wax models and leave it in pieces?"

"No." Steven chortled. "It's what they say in England. It means swell or terrific."

"Swell? You mean, to grow big and fat as a balloon, like this?" He puffed out his beautiful chest, the evil creature, filled his cheeks with air and grimaced comically at my daughter, who collapsed into such a fit of giggles that I was afraid she might wet herself.

Oh, he could charm apples off the tree without even trying. But then, why did that surprise me? After all, I'd learned it within seconds of meeting him myself, a long time ago.

My inner turmoil must have shown, because Brian leaned close and whispered, "Relax, honey, and have another glass of wine. He's not going to spirit our boy away under cover of his dinner napkin."

But although my son might be safe, how could I relax when being in the same room with Marco, close enough to touch him, unraveled me in ways I hadn't expected?

I saw how attentively he listened to Steven and Grace, the respect with which he answered their questions about Italy. I noticed the changes the years had wrought in him, the flecks of silver in his hair, the faint grooves beside his mouth. I saw longing and regret in the glances he occasionally turned my way, and felt an alarming response tug at me. We had started out so full of dreams and hope, but only now did I realize how much we'd been cheated of.

I couldn't wait for the evening to end—and some sort of equilibrium to restore my common sense. When the meal was finally finished, I hoped the worst was over and breathed a premature sigh of relief as we returned to the lobby.

"Goodbye," he said, shaking hands with both children. "I've very much enjoyed meeting you. A pity our time together was so short."

To my unspeakable dismay, Steven said, "Well, it doesn't have to be. There's still tomorrow and you could spend it with us. That'd be okay, wouldn't it, Mom?"

"I'm sure Marco has other plans," I choked out.

"No, he doesn't. He already told us he was going skiing, and you said we were, too. Why can't we do it together?"

I could come up with a dozen reasons, none of which I dared voice. I was afraid a stranger might remark on his resemblance to Marco. Afraid Steven himself might notice it and wonder why he looked more like a man he'd only just met than the one he'd lived with all his life. He might pick up on the invisible net of tension between me and Marco. I wasn't sure I could carry off a whole day of pretending everything was all right when everything was wrong. I was dragging my children into the web of lies and secrets and heartache that were mine alone to bear.

A tense silence spun out as I struggled to come up with a logical refusal to what was, after all, a perfectly reasonable request. I flung Brian a desperate silent plea to bail me out. His answering shrug plainly said, *Your call, honey, not mine.*

I switched my attention to Marco, praying he'd have the decency to step forward and put an end to what he had to know was an impossible dilemma for both of us. But he was watching his firstborn and the naked hunger in his eyes touched me where I was most vulnerable. He'd already lost so much, suffered so much, and we had too much history between us for me to add to his pain.

"If that's what you'd like," I heard myself say, against my better judgment, to be sure, but very much in tune with my heart.

Steven broke into a grin. "Smashing!"

But Marco pretended an interest in the strangers surrounding us, his jaw clenched, precisely as it had been twelve years ago, when he'd stood on the platform in Florence and watched the train take me away from him.

"Tomorrow morning, then. Nine o'clock on the beginners' slope," Brian said, ushering us toward the stairs.

Steven was bubbling with enthusiasm. "He's smashing, Dad. When did you meet him?"

Once again, Brian steered a narrow path between truth and lies. "During the war," he replied and left it at that.

I peeked over my shoulder. Marco stood exactly where we'd left him. Our eyes met, held. He dipped his head in slow acknowledgment. *"Grazie,"* he mouthed.

FOR MOST OF the next day, things weren't as bad as I'd feared. Being in a crowd eased the awkwardness that had been so palpable at dinner, and ski goggles did much to disguise any resemblance between Steven and Marco.

Although we were together, we were also apart, with no need for social interaction. An excellent skier, Marco spent most of the morning helping the children perfect their turns until, by afternoon, they were ready for a greater challenge than the beginners' slope offered.

"They can handle it," he said, forestalling my objection when they begged me to let them tackle a more difficult run.

"What if they find they can't?"

"I promise you, they will be perfectly safe."

Your promises don't amount to a whole lot lately, I almost said. *You wouldn't be here now if they did.*

"Yeah, Mom," Steven cut in. "We're not babies anymore."

"And we'll all be there to run interference if they have problems," Brian added, the subtext of his words escaping our children.

Outvoted on all sides, I again went along with the suggestion. And again, it appeared that my fears were unfounded—until we lined up for the last lift of the day, and Marco and I became separated from Brian and the children.

I'd done my best to stay as far away from him as possible, even to the point of refusing to make more than minimal eye contact. No more covert glances laced with lust, I promised myself. Yet there I was, isolated on a chairlift next to him, with no means of escape, while below us, Brian and the children stopped to wave as they started down to the base of the hill.

When we reached the top, Marco guided me toward a steeper trail than the one they'd chosen. "If we take this run, we'll catch up with them at the halfway point."

"I'm not sure about that," I said doubtfully. "It looks a bit beyond me."

"I'll go first. Just stay in my tracks and you'll be fine."

He made it look easy, but within a hundred yards I wasn't fine at all. Since there was no going back, I had to go forward. The narrowness of the run permitted neither mistakes nor room for the cautious progress that was my stock in trade. After one particularly difficult turn, I hit a patch of ice and hurtled out of control toward him.

He braced himself against the impact. I crashed into him, poles flying. His skis slid backward as he fought to stop me, and his strength and expertise alone prevented us both from ending up wrapped around a tree. Instead he managed a sort of reverse snowplow and I ended up in his arms.

In his arms!

Horrified, I tried to back away, but he held me fast. "I told you this was too difficult for me, but you already knew that, didn't you?" I blasted, punctuating my words by slamming my gloved fist hard against his chest. "It's what you've been after all along, isn't it? You've used my children to get your hands on me, never mind that I have a husband, a good decent man who trusts me—not that you'd know anything about *that,* since you've got a wife but don't have any problem at all making a play for somebody else's. No wonder she left you! No wonder—"

I was shrieking, advertising my misery to the whole mountain. He silenced me by grasping my flailing hands and very gently kissing me, leaving his eyes open and staring into mine as if he searched for my soul.

Perhaps he'd never intended to let things go further than that, but adrenaline and solitude make for a lethal combination. We were both fighting to breathe, and if his heart wasn't racing like a runaway train, mine more than made up for it.

The immediate danger of my falling and breaking a

leg might be past but as the white, silent world of the Alps again settled around us, a more lethal threat took its place. He released my hands and brought his arms around me again and lowered his head and kissed me a second time, slowly and deliberately, renewing acquaintance with my mouth in excruciating, intimate detail.

Although our kisses were more than enough to revive the passion between us, which had never really died, they didn't begin to satisfy it. We clung to each other, and the heat between us would've melted the polar ice cap, let alone the snow beneath our feet. I do believe that if it hadn't been for our skis, we'd have been rolling on the ground in seconds. Our mouths and tongues stole from each other. We said things. Forbidden things.

"I have missed you," he murmured, his lips tracing a frantic path over my face. "I love you. I always will."

"Me, too," I whispered, collapsing against him.

"I won't let you go again."

"You must! We can't..."

Panting, he rested his forehead against mine, and we stood in each other's arms for a while. Then he put me from him. "You're right. We can't."

He secured my loosened bindings and moved behind me so that his skis bracketed mine. "We'll take it slowly the rest of the way," he said, and looping one arm around my waist, steered me safely to where the trail widened. I managed the last half mile to the base under my own steam and without incident.

A light snow was falling, and the area was almost deserted. "Brian and the children must have headed back to the hotel already," I said.

"It would seem so, yes," he agreed, stepping out of his skis and strapping them together.

"Will you have dinner with us again?"

"No."

"Don't you want to say goodbye to Steven?"

"No."

"Why not?"

His eyes met mine. "Because I don't know how," he said.

I started to cry.

He touched my cheek. *"Arrivederci, amore mio,"* he said softly, then propped his skis on his shoulder and without another word, turned and left me.

I watched him go, his silhouette blurred by snowflakes and my tears. And I knew with futile resignation that this would mark the return of the aching, remorseless misery I'd endured the first time I lost him.

CHAPTER ELEVEN

THE CAPTAIN'S VOICE coming over the intercom, announcing their final approach to London's Heathrow Airport, jolted Carly back to the present. She'd become so wrapped up in her grandmother's story, she'd hardly noticed how quickly the hours had passed. Still, she was glad of the interruption. She could hear the tears in Anna's voice and feel them thick in her own throat. If this was what great love did to people, she'd be happy to give it a miss. There was already enough suffering in the world.

"Let me help you, Gran," she murmured, noticing how Anna's hands trembled as she struggled to restore order to her letters and put them back in their folder.

Emotionally exhausted, Anna nodded, laid her head against the back of her seat and closed her eyes. *If Mom was here, she'd be saying I told you so,* Carly thought, *and given the way Gran was looking now, I'd have to agree with her.*

"Have I bored you, darling?" Anna asked, her eyes still closed. "Are you tired of listening to me ramble on?"

"No," she said, and it was true. Somewhere over the Atlantic, her resentment had melted into grudging sympathy for the man she'd initially viewed as the enemy.

Not that she was willing to forgive him for turning her grandparents' marriage into a triangle, but she could no longer fault him for it, either. Fate had played a dirty trick on all of them, and she couldn't wait to learn how they'd dealt with it.

Not tonight, though. Even if they cleared customs quickly and the chauffeured car they'd ordered was waiting to whisk them to their hotel, it'd be at least another hour before she could get Anna to bed for the night. Tomorrow would be soon enough to hear the rest.

I AWAKE to a cool English morning and breakfast served in our hotel room. Carly pretends to be busy pouring tea, but I know she's watching me and wondering if I can cope with another day of travel. But already I feel the warm, fragrant air of Tuscany calling me, filling this old body of mine with new energy.

"Remind me again when our flight leaves this afternoon," I say.

"Not until two. We'll be in Florence by five, except it'll be six there, because they're an hour ahead of us."

"Then I'd better get on with my story. There's a lot left to tell."

"As long as you feel up to it, Gran, I'm ready to listen."

I take a sip of my tea, and with my letters handy, begin, knowing the most difficult years lie ahead and that I must tread delicately over some parts. "I have virtually no memory of the early months of 1952," I tell Carly. "The first time I lost Marco, I'd been a girl, young enough to be forgiven for making mistakes and selfish enough to expect those around me to indulge me in my grief.

"Now, I was a woman, and no longer entitled to that luxury...."

My children needed their mother, and in his own way, Brian needed his wife. He was close to finishing his post-graduate studies. By summer's end, he had to complete his thesis and prepare for his orals. He could do without the added pressure of wondering if I'd turn into the clinging, desperate teenager he'd rescued almost thirteen years before. However distraught I might be, I owed it to my family to cope.

A twofold attack was the best route to take, I decided. First, I had to keep too busy to have time to wallow in misery. So, more than ever before, I devoted myself to my children, attending their every extracurricular activity, taking them to the library, the theater, even to London to cheer on the Cambridge Blues in the annual Oxford-Cambridge boat race. Not that our support counted for much that year. The Oxford boat sank, leaving Cambridge the uncontested winner. But the change of scene did the three of us good. We spent the night in a hotel near Piccadilly Circus, went to a matinee on Sunday afternoon and caught the train back to Cambridge by early evening.

The second part of my plan was more difficult, but also more crucial. I had to enforce stricter limitations on my relationship with Marco. This was something I realized with the arrival of a letter he sent, a few days after we returned from Switzerland.

I am home in body, he wrote, *but in mind and spirit, I am with you and our son, my dearest Anna. The hours we spent together, too few by far but so much more than I ever dreamed we'd share, make even the most tedious days more bearable. Did I remember to thank you for being the best mother a boy could wish for? Did I tell you that you are beautiful? Do you know how much I love you, and that not an hour passes that I don't miss you?*

Miles separate us, amore mio, *but our son was conceived in a love that defies both time and distance, and nothing can ever change that.*

I sat down and fired off a response by return post.

Please stop trying to seduce me any more than you already have. It serves no purpose except to make us wish for what we can't have, and leaves us dissatisfied with what we've got. I can't speak for your marriage, Marco, but you've met my husband and seen for yourself what a fine and honorable man he is. I refuse to insult him by conducting a long-distance love affair with you. If I've misled you into thinking differently—and in my heart, I know I have—then I regret it deeply. I understand your need, and even your right, to play some sort of role in Steven's life. I'm asking you to be equally understanding when I tell you that you can have no part in mine.

I didn't hear from him again until March. His response was brief and to the point.

Firenze
March 4, 1952
Dear Anna,
Your letter served as a timely reminder that for a man to lose his self-respect is to strip him of all that makes him a man. I am not proud of my actions our last day in Switzerland. I betrayed not just your trust, but your husband's, and for that I am sincerely sorry.

I cannot tell you that I will stop loving you because I know very well from years of having tried that it will never happen. What I can and will do is promise never again to burden you with that knowledge, nor will I seek another attempt to ambush you as I did at Christmas. You are my only link to Steven and I will do nothing to weaken it.

I wish you nothing but happiness and good fortune, Anna, and thank you again for letting me into my son's life, albeit only a little and, of necessity, from afar. Be assured that, like you, I put his welfare first and I eagerly await further news of him.

Yours,

Marco

I can't say I was happy after reading this, but I was at peace. Marco and I would always love each other, but our association could not continue unless we honored the ground rules that made it possible.

SPRING ARRIVED, with daffodils and forsythia blooming in the gardens, and the willow trees veiling the banks of the Cam in misty green. Steven joined an outdoor club. Grace danced a solo at her ballet academy's final concert before the summer break.

On June 12, we threw a big party to celebrate Steven's birthday and to say goodbye to all his friends. Fifteen boys showed up with gifts ranging from books about Cambridge and England, to a rugby shirt, to a framed photograph of him with his soccer team, which all the players had signed.

I served fried chicken Maryland-style and potato salad,

and angel food cake. The boys were thrilled to be eating what they considered to be real American food. Before they left, we got them to write their addresses in Steven's new address book, and made them promise to keep in touch.

Later in the month, Brian successfully defended his thesis before the examining body appointed by the university. Confident that my life was back on an even keel, I began preparing for our return home in September.

At the beginning of August, Steven went camping with his club. He'd never spent any appreciable time away from us before and I struggled to loosen the apron strings. But my boy was growing up fast, so rather than embarrassing him in front of his friends by making a fuss, I didn't smother him with hugs and reminders to brush his teeth and eat his vegetables. Instead I settled for a quick goodbye kiss when I dropped him off at the bus station, then went home without looking back.

"It's not forever," Brian teased when he caught me moping that night. "He'll be home in two weeks."

In fact, he never came home again. Late the following Friday, we received word that an upset stomach, which hadn't seemed serious when it first struck, had taken a more critical turn. Steven had developed a high fever and was complaining of a severe headache and sore muscles.

He was brought back to Cambridge by ambulance that same night and hospitalized. By then, he'd lapsed into a coma. The diagnosis was infantile paralysis, known in later years as polio.

We'd heard of this disease, of course. Epidemics among children were common, especially in the summer months. We knew it was an infectious viral disease that could result in paralysis, and was most often transmitted through the mouth as the result of insanitary conditions.

"But kids can recover from it, can't they?" Brian asked the doctors.

"Yes," they said gravely. "In fact, they usually do."

I heard the unspoken *but* in their voices and my mother's instinct told me that my beautiful boy was not going to be one of those children. I was right. The virus had invaded his central nervous system. He died four days later of uncontrolled infection of his entire brain.

It's strange, the things a person latches on to at such times—the trite, insignificant things. Perhaps it's nature's way of protecting us until we're able to confront the awful finality of death. "I never got to say goodbye," I said dully as I sat with my husband on a bench in a nearby park, after leaving the hospital. "I let him go off to camp without telling him how much I love him and how proud of him I've always been."

Red-eyed from weeping, Brian put his arms around me. "He knows that, honey."

It was one of those brilliantly blue and perfect days that sometimes happen in England. Across the park, men in white were playing cricket. The click of the ball as it hit the bat mingled with the polite applause of those watching from the shade of a majestic oak.

"How does God do this?" I asked. "How does He take a child away from his mother and not make the world go dark?"

"I don't know," Brian said brokenly. "Anna, honey, there are things we have to do, phone calls, telegrams—"

"Where's Grace?"

"The Watsons are taking care of her."

Frank and Lilian Watson lived next door, in the other half of our semidetached. Grace and Iris, their daughter, had become friends not long after we landed in England. "That's kind of them," I said. "We must remember to send them a thank-you note."

"They want to help any way they can. Honey, have you given any thought to the…arrangements?"

"I don't think we should expect our parents to come over. It's too far and there's nothing they can do."

"What about Marco? He should be told…."

"Yes."

"Do you want me to call him?"

"Yes."

"It'll come as a terrible—"

"I want to go home now, Brian," I interrupted. "I want to see Grace. I don't want her to hear about her brother from someone else."

Word of Steven's death had preceded us. Neighbors on both sides of the street had drawn their drapes as a token of respect for our bereavement. As the taxi drew up outside our house, mothers appeared at their own front doors and quietly ushered their children inside, as if we might consider the sound of young laughter an affront when it was, in fact, the sweetest music in the world to a parent's ear.

After letting me into the house, Brian went next door to collect Grace and brought home a chicken casserole and a damson pie. "Lilian would've invited us to stay with them for dinner, but figured we'd want to be alone."

Grace hovered in the open back door, her eyes darting anxiously between her father and me. "I heard Gillian Coombes tell Iris that Steven's dead. He's not, is he?"

Someone needed to tape Gillian Coombes's mouth shut, I thought, and felt something give inside me, like a hairline crack on fine porcelain.

Before it could spread and cause irreparable damage, I sat at the kitchen table and drew my child—my only child now—onto my lap. "Yes, sweetie, he is."

She burst into tears. "But I don't want him to be!"

I heard Brian's muffled sob as he turned and stumbled into the back garden. "None of us do, baby," I said, stroking her hair. "None of us do. But he was too sick for the doctors to help him, so God took him to heaven."

An old, tired cliché, perhaps, but I grasped it because it was the only reason I could offer for so swift and merciless an end to a life that had barely begun.

I'm not sure how we got through the rest of that day. I remember we tried to do justice to Lilian's chicken, but ended up throwing it out. We decided to wait until the next day to contact our parents, and also decided a phone call was better than a telegram. I bathed my little girl, tucked her into bed and sat with her until almost midnight.

"You have to get some rest, too," Brian said, leading me to our room after she finally fell asleep from sheer exhaustion. "You're going to need all your strength to get through the days ahead."

I recall lying next to him, still not having shed a tear. I waited until he was asleep, then got up and went across the landing to Steven's room. All his birthday gifts were lined up on his dresser, ready to be packed up for the trip home. His soccer ball sat at the foot of his bed.

Some time later—it might have been minutes or hours—Brian found me standing by the window. "He forgot to take his diary with him," I said conversationally. "I wonder if he noticed?"

"Anna..." Anxious, uncertain, he'd tried to lead me away. "You're scaring me, honey."

"Why? I'm perfectly fine."

"You're in denial."

"No, I'm not."

"Yes, you are. We've lost our son and—"

"You think I don't know that?"

"And it's okay to cry and be angry," he went on patiently. "You'll feel better if you let it out."

But I was encased in blessed numbness, that tiny hairline crack I'd detected earlier well protected from spreading. "What good will that do?" I asked. "It won't change anything. It won't bring him back. Go to bed, Brian. I'm going to sit here by the window and watch the sun come up."

I continued like this most of the next day, an automaton going through the necessary motions, saying what was expected of me when people phoned or stopped by.

...No, Momma. No point in your coming. We'll be home in a few weeks....

...Thank you for your kind words, Headmaster. Yes, we were very proud of him, too....

...His favorite hymn? "All Things Bright And Beautiful." Appropriate, don't you think....

...So thoughtful of you, Professor Milne. Please thank Mrs. Milne for the lovely flowers....

...We don't need more flowers, Brian. Send them to the hospital....

"It's as if she's sleepwalking," I overheard Brian tell

Lilian, when she came at his request to take Grace next door. "If I didn't know better, I'd say I'm more broken up about Steven than she is. She's damming everything up inside, but sooner or later she's going to fall apart, and I don't want Grace here when it happens. She's upset enough as it is."

Shortly after six o'clock that evening, he and I were in the back garden when the doorbell rang, which it had done most of the day, with flower deliveries and friends, neighbors and colleagues coming by with cards and food and sympathy. Expecting more of the same, I let Brian answer.

I was vaguely aware of the murmur of deep voices, of the sound of the front door closing again. Of footsteps coming through the house and along the cinder path edging the lawn, stopping just short of where I sat in a canvas deck chair, facing the river.

I saw a shadow fall across the grass. Felt a hand take mine and draw me to my feet. I looked up and saw Marco. Saw in his eyes an agony beyond bearing.

"Oh, Marco," I whispered, "we've lost our boy." And that dam Brian had spoken of burst its banks in a wrenching, endless flood of tears.

Marco took me in his arms and held me fast. His chest heaved; his breath shuddered. I clung to him because he was all that stood between me and a precipice of despair so deep, I knew if I fell into it, I'd never be able to climb out.

I clung to him because he and I had made Steven and perhaps, if I held on long enough, between us we could give him life again.

Instead, exhaustion eventually took its toll and left me with nothing but the dry, hiccuping aftermath that follows such an emotional bloodletting. Stepping back a pace, I said, "When...did you hear?"

"Brian phoned me this morning. I came as soon as I heard."

"You flew?"

"Yes."

"I'm glad you're here. You should be here. Steven's your son."

"And you are his mother." He paused, and although his voice was steady, I saw that his face was wet with tears. "You have decisions to make, Anna, and they cannot be put off."

He was talking about the funeral. About putting our beautiful boy in the cold, dark earth. About never seeing him again.

It had to be done.

I clenched my teeth to stave off another wave of anguish. "Help me, please," I begged.

He took my hands in his. "Of course I will. I could not be with you when you brought him into this world, my love, but I will stay by your side now. We will say goodbye to him together."

I lifted my face and kissed his cheek. Tasted the salt of his tears, of mine. "I am so glad," I whispered, "that you were with us in St. Moritz. So glad you had those few precious hours with him."

He didn't answer. He put his arms around me and pulled me close again, and let that be enough. We understood each other. We always had. There was no need for words.

I HEAR A NOISE and glance up to see that Carly is struggling to suppress a sob. "Don't cry," I say. "It all happened many years ago."

"But you and Marco had already lost so much. It wasn't fair that you had to lose Steven, too...."

"Life isn't always fair, darling, and there's nothing in this world as cruel or heartrending as a parent having to bury a child. It is absolutely contrary to the order of nature. The young grow old, and then they die. But when fate steps in and decides differently, we have no choice but to seek comfort in the rituals of death."

We chose a sympathetic minister and hoped that his faith in the hereafter would rub off on us. *Thy kingdom come, Thy will be done....*

He told us not to be afraid, that God was merciful. *Yea, though I walk through the valley of the shadow of death, I shall fear no evil for Thou art with me....*

We chose a plot of ground, a casket, flowers. Of all the words in the English language, we struggled to choose those which best defined our love, our loss, our grief, but there weren't any. In the end, we chose a plain gray granite headstone inscribed simply,

Steven Wexley
Beloved son and brother
June 12, 1940–August 11, 1952
"God gives us love. Something to love He lends us."
Alfred Lord Tennyson

We leaned on others to give us strength.

I leaned on Marco throughout those difficult days and for all those difficult decisions, not because he was Steven's biological father, but because he was *there,* a vital emotional support whenever I needed it. But once assured that the proper arrangements were underway, Brian...well, he seemed to disconnect himself from us.

I didn't doubt that he grieved. It was in his eyes, his voice, for anyone to see and hear. Yet when a family most needs to be together, he took refuge at the college. Was it because burying himself in his work helped blunt the edges of his sadness? Did he remove himself from the house because witnessing my pain exacerbated his own and made it too hard to bear? Or was it that he felt three was a crowd and he was the outsider in this tragedy?

Whatever the reason, Marco was the one who held me when I cried. He was the one who sat with me at night when I couldn't sleep, who made me eat and tended to my poor, solitary little daughter. His strong arm prevented me from almost collapsing at the graveside.

Every one of the boys who'd come to Steven's birthday party came to his funeral, too. Subdued, polite, they approached me one by one and offered their sympathy, some with an eloquence beyond their years, and others not able to do more than mutter *I'm sorry.*

They destroyed me with their loyalty, their sweet sincerity. Marco saw how they affected me and steadied me with a hand at my waist. And when he finally went back to Italy, our letters were my lifeline, the one thing that held me back from the brink of hopelessness and despair and the terrible, wrenching guilt that hounded me.

...I knew how those outdoor camps operate, primitively, without adequate bathroom facilities, and enough children have died from infantile paralysis for me to be aware of the risks. I should have warned him. Those men in charge aren't

to blame. Steven was my responsibility, not theirs. His mother, the one person he should have been able to rely on, let him down. It's my fault he died, Marco.

No one is to blame, Anna, least of all you. You gave him everything of yourself, as good mothers do. You filled his life with joy and love. How many of us can say we've been as lucky?

Next week, we're returning to the States. I spent this afternoon at his grave, planting daffodil and hyacinth bulbs, to tell him, when spring comes, that I haven't forgotten him. Once, I couldn't wait to leave England, but now a part of me will always be here, with him, just as another part will be with you. How do I leave you both?

You will not leave us, my dearest Anna. You will carry us in your heart, as I carry both of you in mine. Someday we will remember our son with gladness and speak of him without tears. Until then my love is yours to use however it might comfort you.

I am with you always.

I KEPT HIS WORDS close when I knelt at Steven's grave the day before we left England and traced my hand over his name and whispered goodbye. They gave me the courage to board the flight back to America. I might not have had much memory of the first half of the year, but the second half I would never forget. I wouldn't have survived, if it hadn't been for Marco.

Once I was settled again, our letters flew back and forth

across the Atlantic with more frequency than ever, ostensibly packed with news, but more subtly laced with the admission that although life might have tried to come between us, death had brought us together in a way that nothing and no one could prevent.

September 20, 1952
My dear Marco,

We've been home over a month now, and although I'm always conscious of the empty place at our table, I'm glad to be back in my own nest. Having my family close is helping me heal, but also made me realize I'd fallen into the habit of expecting others to tread softly around me because of my loss. Seeing how our parents have aged in the last two years came as a shocking reminder that I'm not alone in my suffering. It's good for them to have Grace nearby, and good for her, too. I'm afraid that, to some extent, she's always lived in her brother's shadow, never more so than in these last weeks, and needs to be spoiled a little. As much for her sake as theirs, we spent our first few days in Newport with both sets of grandparents.

When we turned into our driveway in Wakefield, our dear Peggy was waiting on the front doorstep to greet us. She had the house sparkling from top to bottom and filled with flowers and the aromas of home-baked bread and apple pie. We shed some tears at seeing one another again, but Grace's delight when Tuxedo came and wound himself around her ankles made us smile again. It was good to see that some things hadn't changed.

We were barely unpacked before Brian once again became caught up in college life. He's been given the promotion he hoped for, as well as a bigger office, and like me, is glad to be back among the familiar. All this makes it difficult for me to understand why, when he's home, he's preoccupied and frequently appears troubled. I've questioned him, wondering if he's ill, but he insists I'm worrying over nothing. I hope so. Despite everything you and I continue to mean to each other, he is very dear to me.

I miss you and ask myself why I wasted so many years keeping you at arm's length when we could have spent them enjoying Steven together. The good memories we lay down are the cushion that gets us through the bad times, and I'm afraid I robbed you of that.

I discovered too late that there are many kinds of love, and no one, least of all a child, should be deprived of one simply because another is in place. How would our son have reacted if I'd told him from the start that you were his father? I used to believe it would undermine his security. Now I wonder if I was wrong, if it would not, in fact, have enriched his too-short life immeasurably. We all live with regrets for the mistakes we make and cannot put right. These, my dear, dear Marco, are foremost among mine.
Forever yours,
Anna

My other regret was that I could do nothing to close the distance that had sprung up between Brian and me. It struck me as especially perplexing because, even as he pulled away from me, our affection for each other and his commitment to us as a family remained strong as ever.

I discovered the reason the next year, six months after our return from England.

CHAPTER TWELVE

HE CAME HOME that night a few mintues after ten. He so often spent the evening working that I no longer waited up for him, and was in bed reading when I heard him come up the stairs. He appeared in the doorway, wearing neither an overcoat nor boots. His hair and shoulders were covered with snowflakes and his shoes sodden. But it was the haggard look on his face that alarmed me the most.

Throwing back the covers, I ran to him and catching his hands, drew him into the room. "For heaven's sake, honey, what happened? You're freezing!"

"I walked home," he said.

"From Kingston, in this weather?"

"It's no more than three miles."

"Why? Did the car break down? Did you have an accident?"

"No."

"But, Brian, it's snowing out. Has been all day."

"Has it?" he said dully. "I hadn't noticed. Anna, we need to talk."

I unbuttoned his suit jacket and stripped it off. Melted snow had soaked through the fabric and left his shirt wet, too. "Whatever it is can wait. You need to get into a hot bath before you catch pneumonia. When did you last eat?"

"I don't remember." He shrugged. "This morning, I guess."

"Then I'm going to fix you something. Come down to the kitchen when you're ready."

He sort of sagged, as if he didn't have the energy to argue, and peeling off his tie and shirt, went into the bathroom. He was a big man, broad like Marco and perhaps an inch taller, but at that moment, he seemed shrunken.

Peggy had made split-pea soup with a ham bone left over from Sunday's dinner. I ladled some into a pot and while it heated on the stove, sliced some of the bread she'd baked to go with it, then made a pot of tea.

Brian came down about half an hour later, looking not quite as pale as before, but still with a bleakness to him that frightened me. He slumped into his chair, pushed aside his bowl of soup and buried his face in his hands.

At a loss, I took a seat across from him and waited. I'd never seen him like this before, not even when Steven died. He was the most unflappable man on earth, and whatever was bothering him had to be huge.

The big old school clock on the wall ticked away the seconds. Finally I could stand it no longer. "Tell me," I said.

He raised his head and faced me. "I've met someone," he said baldly. "I've fallen in love."

CARLY LOOKS utterly shocked, and I wish there was some way I could omit this part of my story, but since it plays such a big part in what comes later, the best I can do is edit the facts. I haven't kept Brian's secret all these years to betray it now and risk tarnishing his granddaughter's memories of him. Needing a moment to decide how best to go on, I ask her to phone down for a fresh pot of tea. While she's doing that, I let the memories rush in....

AT BRIAN'S WORDS, my pulse jumped. "There's another woman?"

"No," he said.

"Then I don't—"

"I'm in love with a man, Anna."

The whole room went still as I struggled to comprehend what he was trying to tell me. "But you're..."

"Unnatural? Immoral? Wrong?" he supplied wearily when I floundered into silence. "Believe me, there's nothing you can call me that I haven't already called myself, a hundred times over. But whatever label you choose, it won't change what I am."

"You're my husband," I said. "You're Grace's father. You love us."

"Yes, I do. And that, too, will never change."

...there are many kinds of love, I'd written to Marco, so sure I had all the answers. But not once had I considered this shadowy, taboo kind that everyone knew existed and no one ever talked about.

"How can you be sure?"

"That I'll always love you?"

"No," I said in a low voice. "That you're in love with...this man."

"How did you know you were in love with Marco?"

"It's not the same thing."

He smiled at me sadly. "Yes, it is, Anna. It's exactly the same thing."

I groped for the edge of the table. Pushed myself out of my chair and went to stare blindly out the window. I thought back to the day he'd come home and asked me about moving to England, the relief he hadn't quite managed to hide when I'd agreed it would be a good idea. He'd said we needed a break from the usual, something to make us appreciate each other more. I'd assumed he was referring to the absence of intimacy between us—without once considering its possible cause.

I remembered his almost obsessive insistence on our doing things together when we got to Cambridge, whether it was being seen as husband and wife at college functions, or watching Steven play soccer on Saturday mornings. And how his enthusiasm had fallen off and we'd slowly drifted back to the old routine, with our address all that had really changed.

I remembered the few occasions I'd initiated lovemaking in the front bedroom of our semidetached, and how, more often than not, it had ended in failure. I'd blamed myself. If a woman couldn't arouse a man to passion, it had to be her fault.

Now, his late nights at the college, here and in England, and the times he didn't come home at all, they made a different kind of sense. A lot of things fell into place that hadn't quite fit before.

I turned back to face him. "How long has this been going on?"

"Months," he said wearily. "Years, I suppose. I just didn't want to admit it."

"Since before you married me? Is that why you did it? So no one would find out?"

"No," he cried. "*No!* It wasn't until after Grace was born that I started having doubts. I told myself I was mistaken, that I was 'normal' and could prove it. Look at my beautiful family, my beautiful wife! But appearances can be deceiving."

Oh, yes. I knew that better than anyone. I'd been living a lie for years. "Has it been the same man all this time?"

"No. I've been attracted to others on and off, but never acted on it. Then I met him, and I realized right away that he was different, even though we never acknowledged how we felt about each other."

"When did you meet?"

"The spring before we went to England."

"Is that why you wanted to accept the Cambridge offer?"

"It was one reason. Professionally, it was a great opportunity, but I also hoped, if I put distance between us, I'd get over him."

"You didn't, though."

He winced, and I had to close my eyes against the wretchedness in his. If ever a man was in hell, with no way out…

"No. We remained in touch the entire time. I dreaded what coming home would mean—being pulled in two directions, lying to you, hurting him. I contemplated suicide, but I couldn't do that to you or Grace. We'd just lost Steven—"

The breath caught in my throat. Not wanting him to see how shocked I was by this revelation, I poured tea into a mug and took it to him. "You've lived with this secret for a long time. What made you decide to tell me about it now?"

"I can't go on like this. It's killing me." He went to touch my hand, then stopped as though, now that the truth was out, I'd be repulsed by him. "What happens next is up to you, Anna. If you want me to move out, or divorce me, I'll understand. I'll leave tonight, if you like."

But I couldn't think that far ahead. All I knew at that moment was that I couldn't stay there, seeing his pain but too enmeshed in my own to care.

"*Tell* me, Anna," he begged.

"What do you want me to say?" I cried, backing toward the door. "That I understand? Well, I don't! I can't! If you had to fall in love with someone else, why couldn't it have been a woman?"

He flinched and turned his face away. Beside myself, I rushed upstairs and spent a sleepless night alone, trying to sort through my emotions. Comparing my situation with his and trying to be fair. Hating that he'd put our safe, respectable lives in jeopardy, and desperately afraid for him. And finally, as the sun rose, accepting that pain is pain, no matter what form it takes or where it strikes. Anguish, torment, self-loathing don't discriminate. They aren't the prerogative of the socially acceptable or the saintly. We each do our best to conform, to be the best that we can be, despite our weaknesses. But at the end of the day, we are what we are.

He came to our room at ten after seven. "I've brought you coffee," he said, setting a tray on the dresser. "And I need to collect a few clothes. The mere sight of me must disgust you, knowing what you now do."

I went to him and slipped my arms around his bowed shoulders. "What I know," I said, "is the agony of loving someone in secret, and I remember very well how you helped me cope with that. You stood by me when I was pregnant and had no one else to rely on. What kind of woman would I be, to repay the favor by deserting you now that you need me?"

"This isn't about me, Anna. It's about what's best for you."

How often, over the years, had he prefaced a remark, a decision, with those very words, and how willingly I'd accepted it as no less than my due!

"Listen to me," I said, cupping his face between my hands. "From a purely practical standpoint, a divorce will benefit no one. We both know society's views on homosexuality. It's not just frowned on in America, Brian, it's illegal. If what you told me last night ever leaked out, it would destroy not only you and your career, but Grace as well. And she's been through enough. So for all our sakes, and because I love you for your kind and gentle soul, I say we do nothing to arouse any sort of suspicion. No divorce, no separate living arrangements, nothing. Publicly we maintain the status quo."

He regarded me from war-weary eyes. "And privately?"

"We lead our separate lives."

"How do we do that, Anna?"

"Discreetly," I said. "Very discreetly, indeed. No one must suspect, least of all Grace."

"Even if we can pull it off, it's a far from perfect deal for you."

"I stopped believing in perfect the day Steven died," I said. "All I know now is that we have to hold on to those nearest and dearest to us, because we can never tell when we might lose them."

"*Carpe diem,* in other words."

"Seize the day, yes."

Later that week, we moved our double bed into what

used to be Steven's room, and replaced it with twin beds in ours, but that was the only outward change we made. As far as the rest of the world was concerned, our lives remained exactly as they always had. Underneath, though, a shift took place in the dynamics of my relationship with Brian that had nothing to do with his falling in love with someone else.

After that night, our roles reversed themselves. For so long, he'd been the one to support me. Taken care of me so willingly, so competently and so lovingly that I'd never had to test the limits of my own endurance. When things went wrong, he fixed them. I could afford to be weak, because he was unfailingly strong.

Not anymore, though. That Brian had actually contemplated suicide told me how close he'd come to the breaking point. What it would've done to Grace, to lose both brother and father within days of each other, shook me more than his other confession. He was my best friend and it was my job now to take care of him, to put him first, for a change.

Confession is supposed to be good for the soul, but it didn't help him. No matter how often I tried to reassure him, he continued to punish himself. He lost weight. Looked gaunt and hunted. His work, which usually brought him such satisfaction, seemed to pall. He was killing himself with guilt as surely as if he'd put a gun to his head. "How can you stand to be in the same room with me?" he once asked.

"Because you're still Brian and I love you," I told him.

I mothered him over the next several months as fiercely, as devotedly as I mothered Grace, and gradually the man he used to be reemerged until, by summer, he was almost himself again.

Whether it was that he finally believed I'd meant it when I said I wasn't interested in a divorce, or whether it had something to do with the other man, I have no idea. He never talked about their association, and I never asked because, in all honesty, I didn't want to know. It was enough that the old Brian was back.

CARLY PUTS DOWN the phone and before she can ask questions that might trip me up, I hurriedly pick up where I left off. She must never guess the whole truth.

"I blamed myself for what had happened. The miracle is that it hadn't happened sooner. After all, I'd been in love with Marco for years, and no husband wants to take second place to another man. Why should your grandfather be any different?"

"But you stayed together anyway."

"Yes."

"Why?"

"For the reasons I explain here," I say, evading a direct answer by taking up the letter I sent to Marco.

Wakefield, Rhode Island
July 27, 1953
Dearest Marco,
First, thank you yet again, not only for your many letters, but for continuing to send them despite my not replying as often as I should. This might have worried you and made you question whether my feelings for you have changed. They have not, Marco. They never will. But other aspects of my life have changed quite dramatically, and I thought

it best to wait until the dust settled before I tried explaining them to you.

Basically what it boils down to is that Brian and I have reached an understanding of exactly what our marriage is really about. I don't imagine it comes as any surprise to you to hear that we haven't lived as husband and wife for several years now. I think you saw for yourself, last summer, that although we share a home and a family, we are in many ways very far apart. Perhaps the saddest proof of this was that, much though we felt each other's pain when Steven died, we weren't able to reach out to each other as most married couples do. I clung to you, and my poor Brian had to carry his grief alone because he was in England, and the person he needed most was here in America.

From this, you've probably guessed that he's in love with someone else. He has been for a long time, in a way that he and I never were, but which you and I understand all too well. I learned of this earlier in the year and although the details of his relationship aren't mine to share, I can tell you we have decided against divorce for a number of reasons, not the least of which is our daughter, Grace. Her brother's death has left her very fragile, and for us to tear apart what remains of her family is unthinkable.

Consequently, on the surface, at least, our marriage is exactly as it's always been. Even Genevieve, who knows me better than anyone else, isn't aware. You might recall my mentioning that her husband fell ill in March, and I'm sorry to say that he died at the end of June. His death hit her very hard and I went to New York for two weeks to be with her. I don't believe she guessed that anything had changed with me.

I won't say it's been easy, but all in all I think it's safe to say Brian and I have adjusted to our new situation without arousing any suspicion among those closest to us. It's no effort for us to to be affectionate because we're sincerely fond of each other, which is, perhaps, our most enduring strength.

Nonetheless, what's happened has made me take stock of my priorities. We become so caught up with doing the "right thing" and abiding by the conventions society imposes on us, that we often forget we're not all cast in the same mold. What matters, I've learned, is recognizing that life is our most precious gift and wasting it, the greatest sin.

Other than that, I have little else to tell you, except that I plan to go to Cambridge next week. The anniversary of Steven's death is coming up and although he's not there anymore in any real sense, I feel a deep need to visit those places holding my last memories of him. Especially, I need to go to his grave and see for myself that it's being well cared for. Originally Brian planned to come with me, but he's decided to stay home and take Grace sailing instead. Like her father, she loves to be on the water, and it'll be good for them to spend a week alone together. He misses Steven terribly, though, and is planning his own pilgrimage later in the year.

And what of you and your daughter, Marco, now

that she's past babyhood? We'll always miss our son, but even though no one else can ever take his place, if you could be as close to Claudia as I am to Grace, I think it might make you less heartsore. Regardless, please take very good care of yourself. You are and always will be very dear to me.

Anna

I hadn't expected to remain untouched by my return to England, but I hadn't expected to be quite so moved when, before bringing the aircraft in for final landing, our pilot flew over London, pointing out via the intercom the famous landmarks. From my window seat, I could clearly see all the places we'd taken the children our first Christmas there: the Houses of Parliament, Westminster Abbey, London Bridge, the Tower, all linked by the murky gray-blue ribbon of the Thames threading east to the sea.

Tears filmed my eyes. Nothing, it seemed, had changed. Yet in the last year, everything had. My son would never again clown with his sister by the fountain in front of Buckingham Palace, pose for a photograph outside Number 10 Downing Street or sprinkle brown malt vinegar on fish and chips served in a thick layer of newspaper. When the plane landed, I was openly sniffling into my handkerchief, much to the consternation of the man sitting next to me. "Are you a nervous flyer, hon?" he asked me kindly.

That night, I stayed in a hotel near Berkeley Square and caught the train to Cambridge the next day. Again, the weather was clear and warm. After checking in at a small guesthouse not far from the colleges, I walked downtown to Market Square with its open-air stalls and bought a mass of dahlias and baby's breath from a flower-seller. Then, I went to the cemetery.

The big iron gates were closed, a sign that no burials were planned that day, but a smaller one stood open for visitors on foot. I passed the caretaker's lodge and up the main path, turning left at the stand of thick shrubs topping a low rise.

Given my reaction before I'd even landed in England, I should have been better prepared for what lay ahead as I reached the willow tree beside his grave. Not that I'd thought for a second it would be easy coming back here. I knew I'd cry, that the grief I assumed was under control would sweep back with renewed cruelty. But nothing I anticipated came close to the swell of emotion that engulfed me when I stood before his headstone. Perhaps nothing ever could.

My baby...my boy...

Suddenly I was on my knees, with the dahlias lying in disarray around me. I spread my hands on the sun-warmed grass that covered him, and my heart splintered into a hundred pieces, and I wept as I had never wept before. Not when I was led to believe Marco had died, not even when I buried my precious boy.

I wept for all the times I'd been too busy or too impatient to listen to him; for every missed chance to look at him and see how beautiful and perfect he'd been. I wept for the things he'd been cheated of: high school graduation, his first kiss, falling in love, the wife he'd never marry and the children he'd never have.

I wept until I was so wrung out, I didn't have a drop of moisture left in me. When at last I lifted my head and sat back on my heels, the sun had dipped behind the willow tree and cast long, graceful shadows over him.

I noticed then that although the grass was neatly trimmed, the spent blossoms from the bulbs I'd planted last year still hung from tired stems. Searching through my purse for the nail scissors in my cosmetics bag, I cut the wilted stems to the ground.

Not far away was a grating with a spigot over it and, as was common in England then, several metal vases that visitors could use for the flowers they brought. "Purple and red were your favorite colors, my sweetheart," I whispered, arranging the dahlias and baby's breath in a tall, sturdy container and placing it near his head.

The first faint breeze of evening stirred the branches of the willow tree in an answering whisper. *Smashing, Mom!*

I kissed my fingertips, traced them over his name, picked up my belongings and left. I was raw inside, but instinct took me to the one place where I might find some ease.

I entered King's College by the North Gate and went to the Chapel. During the academic term, choral services were held most evenings, but not during the summer months, and I had the place to myself.

Slowly I walked the length of the nave, as far as the six-teenth-century oak screen beyond which lay the chancel. My glance drifted from the ornately carved choir stalls and came to rest on the altar. Behind it stood Reuben's *Adoration of the Magi,* with the magnificent stained glass of the East Window above it, and for a moment I could almost hear the faint echo of boy sopranos singing "Once In Royal David's City."

My throat ached. So many memories…

Swallowing, I slipped into the end seat of the first pew and sat, letting the holy silence of that special place seep into my bones. At some point, a man in black robes appeared briefly. A short while later, the subdued strains of the organ filled the air.

When I was finally ready to leave, the sun was low, leaving the Chapel dusted with cool shadows, but sufficient light remained for me to see that I was not, after all, the only visitor. As I turned to go back down the aisle, a man rose from the last row of chairs.

It was Marco.

CHAPTER THIRTEEN

TEARS ARE STREAMING down Carly's face. "I knew he'd come, and I'm so glad!"

"I was, too, precious. I walked into his arms and let his strength envelop me."

"What did you say?"

"At first, nothing. All that mattered was that we were together again. Eventually, linking hands, we left the Chapel by the South Porch. On one side was the Front Court; on the other, the Gibbs Building where your grandfather had spent so many hours on his research."

Still without speaking or even exchanging glances, we'd turned west by mutual accord and walked along the footpath down to the river. The setting sun gilded the water and bathed us in its dying glow.

Daring at last to look at him, I saw that, like me, he was hard-pressed to contain his emotions. They say that the eyes are the windows of the soul, and if this is true, his were awash in a grief every bit as stark as mine.

"You're really here," I said, my voice thick with tears. "I can't believe it."

"You really imagined I'd let you make this pilgrimage alone, my love?"

"I hoped you wouldn't, but I didn't want to pressure you. That's why I was deliberately vague in my letter."

"I'd already decided I had to be here, even before I heard your plans. Like you, I felt a need to visit our son today. And like you, *carissima,* I found it a profoundly moving experience."

"What do you mean, *like me?* Are you saying you saw me at the cemetery this afternoon?"

"*Si.* I waited for you since early this morning because I knew his grave was where you'd be."

"Why didn't you show yourself?"

"I intended to. But then I saw how stricken you were and held back. It was not my right to intrude on such a private moment. I'd already poured out to him all that is in my heart. Now it was your turn to be alone with him. I waited until you were about to leave, then stepped out from behind the tall headstone where I'd hidden. You passed so close by me, I could have reached out my hand and touched you. But your eyes were blinded with pain, and you weren't ready for me to reveal myself." He gave me an apologetic glance. "Once again, I've stooped to spying on you, *carissima.* It was no coincidence that we met in the Chapel. I followed you there."

"But you still didn't come forward."

He lifted his shoulders in the merest shrug. "I could see you were a woman who needed comfort beyond anything I could offer."

"And now?"

"Now, we help each other." A fleeting smile touched his mouth. "And I'm a man, my Anna, not a saint. My patience had worn thin." He gazed at me searchingly. "Are you angry with me? Do you want me to leave?"

I stopped in the middle of the river walk and faced him, forcing others out for an evening stroll to step aside and skirt around us. "No," I said. "I'm not angry. Of all the people in the world, you're the only one I want to be with today." And uncaring of who might see us, I reached up and kissed him.

He tasted of relief, and hunger sternly held in check. He tasted like the man I'd kissed when I was eighteen.

We drew apart reluctantly, a couple in their thirties behaving like love-starved teenagers which, in many ways, is what we were. The silence between us that of two minds in perfect harmony, we continued walking, wrapped in the distinctive flavor of an English summer—of trees in full leaf and neatly trimmed lawns and laundry dried in the sun.

With twilight deepening, we came to a picturesque riverside inn and sat at a scarred wooden table in the dining room. We ate tenderloin of lamb in red-currant sauce, and drank lager and lime because the wine selection was nonexistent and neither of us cared for the heavy English beer.

For the first time since 1939, we had the luxury of talking to each other at leisure and without reservation, filling in the diary entries of our lives which, for one reason or another, we hadn't shared sooner.

"How has it been for you, this last year?" he began as we waited for our meal.

"Unbearably hard. Whenever I think I'm getting past it, it hits me again." I sighed, the tears that struck out of nowhere, the sudden grief brought on by some small, unexpected incident, crowding my mind. "The little things are the worst, like the time I unpacked one of the boxes we'd put away before we came here and found his train set and his old teddy bear and his baby pictures."

And later, as we lingered over our drinks, I told him how Genevieve and Brian had stood by me when they'd learned I was pregnant; of my hasty wedding and that neither my parents nor my in-laws had ever made an issue of Steven's early birth. I described my wedding day, with everyone assuming my tears sprang from joy when, in fact, they were for Marco because I believed he was dead.

In turn, he told me more about *his* decision to marry; he said he'd hoped to feel more complete, but instead had ended up emptier than ever.

"Does your wife know about me?" I asked.

He shook his head. "You're mine alone, not to be shared."

"Perhaps she sensed that she had a rival. Perhaps that's why you weren't able to make it work between you."

"I did my best. She did, too. But ours was never a love match and we both recognized that from the start."

"Do you still pretend to live together?"

"No. Last Christmas, she moved back with her parents for good, although, in truth, she never really left there. I sold our apartment, and this spring converted the floor above the firm's offices into a place for myself."

"What about Claudia?"

"I'm lucky if I see her more than an hour or two a week, mostly because I insist on it."

"But you're entitled to visit your daughter, Marco. Why don't you apply to the courts for reasonable access?"

"Because in Italy, a man chooses a wife primarily as a mother for his children. If love also happens, that's a blessing. If it does not, where he sleeps and keeps his clothes is immaterial, as long as he does nothing overt to destroy his family's unity."

"That's why you had me send letters to your office?"

"Partly, but also because there was nothing of Giulia in that place. It was always yours and mine."

"But I was never there with you."

"You are everywhere, Anna," he said. "You fill every corner of my life."

We talked then about despair, and wanting to give up. About duty and obligation and hope that never really died. And I realized that, of the two of us, I'd made by far the better bargain.

I'd been cherished. I'd known happiness, even if it had always contained an edge of regret, of sorrow. I'd enjoyed a measure of contentment with a husband who'd loved me as deeply as he could.

I'd known the quiet joy of tucking my babies into bed at night and watching them sleep, of kissing away their little hurts and being the guardian of their most treasured secrets. I'd seen their faces light up at the first snowfall, their delicious anticipation on Christmas Eve. I'd been mother, teacher, nurse, advocate; reader of bedtime stories, tooth fairy and stealthy Santa Claus.

All this, and much more, I related to Marco, occasionally making us both smile and even laugh, which I'd never have believed possible on this of all days. "It's how Steven deserves to be remembered," Marco said, when I remarked on the fact.

But the knowledge that constantly lurked in my mind was that memories were now all I had left of my boy. It must have betrayed me because, when the dining room closed and we had to leave, Marco said, "Let me be with you tonight, Anna. Let me hold you, just for a little while. Let me comfort the mother of my son."

"Yes," I said. "Please."

He inquired about accommodation at the inn, and we were shown up a narrow staircase to a room tucked under the eaves. It held a double bed, a straight-backed chair and a small dresser. The bathroom was at the end of the hall.

I had nothing with me but the clothes on my back and a few cosmetics in my purse. No change of underwear, no toothbrush, no glamorous nightgown. Yet I had everything I needed, to find the peace I'd been afraid would elude me that night.

I went to the window and watched the moonlight glimmering on the slow-moving river. Coming up behind me, Marco loosened my hair from its prim chignon and ran his fingers through it. "When I was in prison, I used to dream of someday doing this again," he murmured.

I felt his lips against the side of my neck, the heat of his mouth against my skin. I turned in his arms and put his hand where my heart beat just below my left breast. "It isn't a dream now," I said. "I'm here, Marco. I'm real."

We undressed each other with leisurely concentration, acknowledging with a touch, a kiss, the changes the years had brought. He had a scar on his shoulder, another on his thigh. His chest was deeper than when I first met him, his waist perhaps not quite as trim.

I'd carried two babies to term, and had a tiny web of faded stretch marks at my navel to prove it. My breasts were not as high, my hips not as narrow. Parts of me that used to be firm tended to jiggle more now. But, "You are the most beautiful woman in the world," he whispered, and I believed him, because to me, he was the most beautiful man.

We slipped beneath the bedcovers and rediscovered

each other slowly. After all these years, time was on our side at last and there was no need for hurry. Afterward, I lay in his arms and listened to him breathing. I felt his eyelashes brush against my cheek when, half-asleep, he kissed me and uttered my name. I felt his arms close tighter around me when I tried to turn over in the bed. And I knew, no matter what the future held, I could face it because nothing would ever come between us again.

THE NEXT MORNING, we took a taxi to the cemetery to collect his rental car. The weather had changed, and it was raining—a brief and gentle summer shower that fell lightly and covered my hair with tiny crystals. We went to Steven's grave again and stood together, each of us wrapped in our own thoughts. I wondered if our son knew that the man at my side was his father.

When we had to go, tears blurred my vision. I hated leaving him there, so alone, so far from all who loved him. I hated the wasted years when he could've known Marco, if I'd been brave enough to defy convention. Yet he'd been luckier than most children whose mothers married the first man who offered to get them out of a tight spot. He'd never experienced rejection, never been on the receiving end of the kind of cruel indifference that might have been his lot. Brian had truly cherished him as one of his own.

"Will it ever get easier?" I sobbed when we were in the car again, with the windshield wipers slapping at the glass.

"Perhaps not," Marco said hoarsely. "Perhaps the best we can hope is that we'll simply become used to the pain. The anger will become resignation. But we'll mourn him the rest of our lives."

We went next to my guesthouse to collect my belongings and pay what I owed, then to his hotel for him to do the same. There was never any question that we'd spend the rest of the week together. "But not," he told me, as we drove away from the city, "here in Cambridge where you might be recognized. I put your reputation at risk once. I won't willingly do it again."

He took the road that led east toward Newmarket, then north and through a sleepy village to another inn, much larger than the one we'd stayed in last night, and much more elegant. Built in the mid-nineteenth century, it stood at the end of a grove of oak trees, in fifteen acres of fields where cattle grazed.

"I came across it while waiting for you to arrive," he said when I asked how he'd learned of the place.

Our room was large, with a four-poster bed, a small sitting area and its own bathroom. Downstairs was a dining room and a bar that opened to a small terrace, beyond which lay the formal gardens.

By then the rain had stopped, so we walked the two miles to the village. "You understand I'll never let you go again, don't you?" Marco said over a plowman's lunch at the local pub.

"Yes, as long as you accept that whatever your arrangement with Giulia, I must stay with Brian because my daughter needs both her parents. Can you live with that?"

"I'd have it differently, if I could. But even if you were single, divorce isn't legal in my country. Perhaps that's why we take such a matter-of-fact view of marriage. But Americans, I suspect, are not quite as pragmatic."

"Some of us are," I said, recalling the night Brian had

unburdened himself to me. "Circumstances force us to be. And I can promise you I wouldn't be here with you now, Marco, if I wasn't absolutely sure I'm exactly where I need to be."

What I remembered most about the days that followed were the unhurried pleasure of us lying in bed with the morning sun striping the room, and talking—or not, as the mood took us. Of making love not with clandestine haste, but with the unselfishness of true intimacy.

I realized that the main reason I hadn't pressed him to join me in Cambridge was that I'd been afraid to test the strength of our love, in case time and distance had tainted it. But it had not grown thin and tired from neglect. Rather, it had aged like fine wine. Grown richer, more full-bodied, more mature. And I knew that nothing could weaken it, not time or distance or outside influences. I could continue to fulfill my roles as mother, wife, daughter, friend, secure in the knowledge that no matter how much of me I gave to other people, my first love would always be my true love.

We spent our last night together in London, and the next morning, he drove me to the airport. Saying goodbye had never been our strong suit, and I was able to hold myself together because I knew he was having as hard a time as I was not breaking down.

"How do I let you leave me?" he muttered against my mouth. "You're everything to me. So I will not say *arrivederci*. Instead I say, until the next time, *carissima. Ti amo.*"

There's no easy method to amputate a limb. It has to be done quickly and cleanly. So I kissed him, then hurried away, turning at the last moment for a final glimpse. He stood as he had the day I left Florence, a solitary figure among the crowd, his gaze fixed on me.

Quick and clean might be the only way to amputate a limb, but preventing the pain that follows is impossible.

WE MET AGAIN every August after that except one, for the next forty-seven years, and always somewhere in Britain or Europe because those places weren't part of our other lives and we could play at being married. As soon as I cleared customs at Heathrow, I'd race down the concourse so fast, my feet hardly touched the ground, and there he'd be, always waiting in the same spot.

Leaving my luggage sprawled wherever it happened to fall, I'd fly into his arms and he'd hold me tight and kiss me as if there was no tomorrow, and I'd say to myself, *At last, I'm home again, back where I belong!*

For the first few hours, the rest of the world ceased to exist. We'd go to the place we always stayed in London, a small boutique hotel in Belgravia. The minute our bedroom door closed behind us, we couldn't get at each other fast enough.

By the next morning, I'd remember the other half of my life—my daughter, my husband, my parents—and be flooded with guilt that I could so easily and thoroughly push them out of my mind, even for a little while. But such was the love I had for Marco. It consumed me. For four weeks a year, I was his wife and he came first.

We always started and ended our month in Cambridge, at Steven's grave. We'd lay flowers in his favorite colors at his headstone and sit quietly beside him. Talk to him, talk about him. Laugh, cry, remember. In between, we'd explore other places, at first confining ourselves to Britain.

We didn't need glamour and bright city lights—although sometimes we had them, too; we needed time. Time to gather all the ordinary and special things married couples do, and weave them into a tapestry of memories to sustain us when we were apart. We danced like honeymooners when we were in our forties and fifties. We made love in elegant hotel suites, remote inns, on the Yorkshire moors, on a secluded beach in North Wales. We sat on a seawall in Penzance and ate warm Cornish pasties. We dined on lobster in Edinburgh.

Once, we rented a cottage in Devon and played house. I baked him an apple pie; he taught me the secret of making really good Alfredo sauce. I ironed his shirts; he cut the grass.

We stuck out like sore thumbs to the locals, betrayed by our accents and clothes as belonging to a more exotic species, but what really set us apart was not how we sounded or looked, but that we never took each other for granted, and we never squandered a single moment of our time together.

We laughed, we loved and we fought.

…*Stop telling me which side of the road we're on. You're not in America now…*.

…*If all you're going to do is complain about how much better the weather is in Tuscany, maybe you should spend next August there…*.

…*I do not snore! How would you know anyway? You were asleep before I came to bed…*.

…*Don't you dare compare me to Giulia!…*

…*You talk too much. Italian wives know when to keep quiet…*.

…*I don't know why I love you. You're the most impossible man I've ever met…*.

...I adore you. I can't live without you....

Brian, my children and my family had taught me there are many kinds of love. But Marco was the one who taught me its enduring power between a man and a woman whose hearts truly are, as he put it, *sincronizzazione*. In unison. In tune.

Love like ours transcended time, distance, culture and even death. It formed an indestructible chain that linked us together forever. We might grow old, lose our looks, our health, but our love never aged, never grew tired. It defied every obstacle life threw at it, and made it possible for me to leave him at the end of August because we carried each other in our hearts.

We never used the word *goodbye* when I had to go. Always, at that last difficult moment, he'd cradle my face between his hands, smile and say, "Until the next time, *carissima. Ti amo.*"

Not an ideal arrangement by most people's standards, perhaps, and certainly far from conventional, but it was the best we could manage without hurting those close to us.

THE YEARS PASSED, some marked by celebration, others by ill-fortune and tragedy. In 1953, Uncle James dropped dead of a heart attack on the golf course, the same year Aunt Patricia was diagnosed with diabetes.

My sweet Grace entered adolescence and fought everything to do with it, especially me. Almost overnight, she changed from a sunny, even-tempered child into a sullen stranger, offhand and defiant.

You can't make me...
I didn't ask to be born....
I'm not Steven. I don't walk on water....

Her litany of grievances against me was endless. Not unusual, I suppose. Most mothers and daughters clash during what are euphemistically referred to as "the difficult years."

"You're a fine one to talk," she once snarled at me, when I called her to task for lying to me.

Brian, who happened to be home, gave her a dressing down unlike any she'd received before. "Don't you *ever* let me hear you talk to your mother like that again," he lambasted her. "You have *no* idea, no idea at all, of the sacrifices she's made to give you a good and loving home."

Stunned that her mild-mannered father would adopt such a harsh tone, she burst into angry tears. "You don't know what she's really like, Daddy. No one does."

When she graduated from high school in 1958 and was accepted into the teacher training program at Rhode Island College in Providence, we'd achieved peace of a sort, but we never quite recovered from those turbulent years. I always sensed a reserve in her after that, a faint disapproval, that saddened me.

Peggy, now a tireless seventy-two, had remained with us, but a broken hip that winter forced her into retirement and she went to live with her eldest son. The next year, Genevieve married for the third time and shocked her mother by wearing black.

"Well, I'm hardly eligible for white, and cream makes me look as if I was taken out of the oven before I finished baking," she told my poor aunt, who'd never quite understood how she'd managed to produce such an irrepressible daughter. "It's all your fault, anyway, Ma. I inherited my fair skin and red hair from you."

On the positive side, she was madly in love with a really nice man who both adored and deserved her.

In late January 1965, my beloved father was killed when his car skidded on black ice and hit a power pole. He was sixty-eight, still practicing law, but looking forward to retiring and spending his remaining years traveling with my mother.

Although she appeared to cope with sudden widowhood, just as she'd coped with every other unkind thing life threw at her, we could see how devastated and lonely she was, so Brian and I invited her to live with us.

In April, his parents retired to Florida. Changes were taking place. The two houses we'd grown up in were sold and had strangers living in them. That summer, Grace completed college and went to teach at a school in Somerset, Massachusetts. In the space of a few months, our family had, in effect, shrunk from eight to half that number, the fourth being Tuxedo who, now that Grace no longer lived at home, transferred his affections to my mother.

Theirs was a love affair from day one. Whether she was dozing on the porch in summer or knitting by the fire in winter, he never strayed far from her side. He slept at the foot of her bed every night and followed her on her walks through the neighborhood.

At forty-nine, Brian decided he'd had enough of the scholarly life and, in partnership with two other avid yachtsmen, opened a sailing charter with bases in Rhode Island and the Caribbean. It meant he was often away, but for the first time in years, he was enjoying life again. Whether it was being free of college politics that did it, or the company he kept, I couldn't say. That was his business.

The one constant in my life was Marco. In addition to

writing each other during the week, we'd talk on the phone for at least an hour every Sunday. He sent me flowers on my birthday, on Valentine's Day, at Christmas and especially, on Mother's Day. And sometimes he'd send me flowers for no reason at all except to tell me he was thinking of me. On those occasions, he chose roses and freesias.

Then, the day before we were to meet in 1968, the pattern we'd established was broken by a phone call from Rudolfo, Marco's partner. Marco had been on-site at a church undergoing architectural restoration that morning and had fallen from the scaffolding. He was hospitalized with a broken leg, and although he wasn't critically injured, he wouldn't be joining me in England that year.

CHAPTER FOURTEEN

ONCE UPON A TIME, I would have fallen apart at such news and expected Brian to pick up the pieces and put me back together again. Not anymore. I'd learned to stand up to life's hard knocks. It would take more than a broken leg to keep me from Marco's side. If he couldn't come to me in England, I would go to him in Italy.

As planned, I flew to London, spent the next day in Cambridge and continued to Florence the day after that. The city I'd fallen in love with hadn't changed significantly in twenty-nine years. Its beautiful churches still dominated the skyline; its *piazze* were still crowded with people sipping campari at outdoor *trattorias*. I stopped for a quick lunch, then went to the hospital where I bought a huge bunch of dark red and deep yellow freesias from a street vendor.

By then, I understood much more Italian than I had at eighteen. Enough to know what was being said when I arrived at the open door to Marco's private room and found he had another visitor, a woman about my age.

"Naturally I came," I heard her say. "You are my husband, after all."

So this was Giulia.

Hovering in the hall, I peered through the crack in the door and took stock of the woman he'd married. She had on a cotton print dress more suited to someone a third her age than a woman nearing fifty, her hair tied up in a ponytail.

My initial surge of jealousy that she wore Marco's ring was mitigated by my unabashed satisfaction at seeing that she was plain and dumpy, with thick ankles and a petulant mouth. I was wearing much better in middle age!

"You needn't have troubled yourself," Marco responded, staring out the window. "As you can see, I'm in very good hands."

"For now. But they tell me you're being discharged on Thursday. What happens then?"

He half turned his head to look at her, a weary smile touching his mouth. "Don't worry, I won't impose myself on you."

"Easy to say, but if you're on crutches—"

"I'll manage, Giulia. Do not disturb yourself on my account."

"Well, I suppose you can stay with your mother."

"My mother is almost eighty," he said, then added pointedly, "and even if she were half that age, *I* am not a child."

She thrust out her lower lip. "Do as you please, then. If there's nothing you need from me, I might as well go."

"There's nothing," he said. "Give Claudia my love."

I moved farther away at that point, to a window overlooking a courtyard, and waited until I saw her leave his room, waddle down the hall and disappear through the swing doors at the far end. He lay with his eyes closed when I returned and my heart seized at the bleakness I saw in his face.

Stepping quietly in my soft-soled shoes, I crossed to his bed, wafted the flowers under his nose, then leaned over him and whispered, "I have something you need," and kissed him.

His eyes opened so wide, I could see twin images of myself in their pupils. *"Dio!"* he breathed. "If I'm dreaming, please don't let me wake up!"

I kissed him again, more lingeringly. "You're not dreaming, my darling."

His arms came around me, strong as ever, and held me fast, and for a while we remained like that, absorbing each other's scent and substance, as we always did when we first saw each other after a year apart. We laughed a little, cried a little and murmured all the incoherent, disjointed nonsense that lovers resort to in an effort to define emotions too vast to be contained by words.

Then, when the first rush of emotion had passed, he released me just enough to look me in the face again. "I am so glad to see you, but you shouldn't be here, Anna. If you'd come five minutes earlier—"

"Yes," I said. "Giulia was here. I saw her. I stood outside your door and heard how she spoke to you, and I wanted to slap her."

"She was being the dutiful wife, doing what's expected of her. Keeping up appearances." He grimaced. "Not that anyone here actually cares."

"I care," I said heatedly. "She won't have to worry that she'll be saddled with taking care of you while you recover. That's my job."

He protested, as I knew he would, but my mind was made up. "We've had a lot of practice at being discreet, my love. If it'll ease your mind, I'll stay away from this hospital room, but when you're discharged, I'll be waiting for you."

His smile told me I'd won him over. "Have you booked into a hotel yet?"

"No. I came straight here. I left my bags at the information desk downstairs."

"Good." He pulled open the drawer in his bedside table and withdrew a set of keys. "Stay at my place—you know the address. I'll call Rudolfo and tell him to expect you. Anything you need, ask him, and when they let me out of here, I'll come to you there. But now, *tesoro*, it's better that you leave. I'm expecting my sisters to stop by later with my mother."

HIS APARTMENT, a long, high-ceilinged loft above his offices, showed me a side of him I'd never had the chance to see. Spare and elegant, it was all clean lines and cool colors, with windows along one wall that gave a view of the river. The bathroom was enclosed. The rest of the area flowed from kitchen to sitting to sleeping space, with bookcases serving as dividers. Not quite a monk's cell—there was too much comfort for that—but hardly a luxury penthouse, either. If I'd been asked, I would've described it as adequate. But it was by no means a home, and that made me sad. He deserved better.

I said as much, three days later, during the first part of our trip north. Since we couldn't risk being seen together in Florence, I'd had to find somewhere else for us to stay, and after mulling it over, I decided that if we couldn't be together in Cambridge, there was only one other place that would do. The train took twelve hours to get there, but we made the journey over two days, and the eight-hour run as far as Zurich on the first day left us ample opportunity to talk.

"Maybe it's exactly what I deserve," he said, when I suggested Giulia had a lot to answer for, running home to mother as she had and leaving him to fend for himself. "Maybe I haven't yet learned how to please a woman."

"You please me."

"Even with my leg in a cast?"

I gave him my best imitation of a leer. "Especially with your leg in a cast. I can really have my way with you now."

"Funny," he said, trying not to smile. "I was under the impression you'd been doing that for years."

We stayed in a hotel near the railroad station that night, had dinner in our room and went to bed early. Although he'd never admit it, I could see the day had wearied him.

"Tomorrow will be better," I promised.

"Not by much," he muttered, the whole idea of relinquishing his independence and having to rely on me clearly an affront to his masculinity. "Your being my nursemaid wasn't on the agenda when we planned this year's trip. I'm going to be about as much fun as a bad case of food poisoning."

"You're alive and you're lying next to me in bed, Marco Paretti," I scolded. "Compared to what could have happened, I'll settle for that."

The next morning, we boarded the train for St. Moritz, arriving there early in the afternoon. And when I saw his smile, I knew I'd chosen well.

We spent three weeks relaxing in the sun by the lake, listening to open-air concerts. We talked about Steven, who would've been twenty-eight had he lived, debating what career he might have chosen and if he would've been married by now.

"We could be grandparents," I said, with a small sense of shock, but a small sense of loss, too. All these years later, a part of me still hurt whenever I thought of our son.

"We probably will be at some point," Marco said. "Just not together."

Each day I saw an improvement in his health. He grew tanned and more gorgeous than ever, with the silver in his hair more predominant now. The strain around his eyes and mouth eased. He laughed more often, more spontaneously.

He was doing well under the care of a local orthopedic surgeon, enough that we devised innovative ways of making love despite the cast on his right leg. Daring, not-talked-about-in-polite-society ways, our grandmothers would have said. But we'd always been ahead of the crowd, and this was the sixties, the era of free love, peace, flower power and letting it all hang out. What used to be taboo was now accepted. We'd finally come into our own.

Too soon, we had to go back to our separate lives. He flatly refused to let me take him back to Florence and instead flew home, arranging for Rudolfo to meet him at the airport. My flight departed an hour before his, and as always, he stayed with me until final boarding was called.

"Until the next time, *carissima*," he said, sticking with our tradition of no tearful, protracted goodbyes. *"Ti amo."*

He'd broken his leg, not his neck, but his accident served as a reminder that we weren't as immortal as we liked to suppose. The realization that, sooner or later, there wouldn't be a next time suddenly hit me hard. I clung to him, sobbing—a cruel thing to do because it upset him terribly.

"What is this?" he murmured hoarsely, holding me close with one arm while balancing both crutches under the other.

"I don't want to leave you," I wept.

"But you never do, my love. You're always with me, no matter how many miles lie between us."

He was always in my heart, too, but I wanted him in my arms. I wanted to see the heat of passion in his eyes when he looked at me. I wanted the house he'd once promised me in Fiesole, wanted him coming home to me every day. I didn't care about growing old, as long as I could grow old with him.

I wanted what I couldn't have.

Swallowing, I drew a shuddering breath and swiped at my tears. "All right," I said, disengaging myself from him, "but promise me you'll take better care of yourself in the future. I don't want you standing me up again next year."

He managed a smile. "It'll take more than a broken leg to keep me away."

I left him then and didn't look back. If I had, I would never have been able to go.

HAD I BEEN of a more superstitious bent, I might have seen Marco's accident as an omen of worse to come and not been quite as blindsided by what happened next. As it was, I came home expecting everything to be as it had always been, and at first, it appeared that it was.

Brian appeared fit and happier than I'd seen him in years, and my mother seemed fine. The next morning, though, as I sat on the back porch enjoying midmorning coffee with her and giving a carefully edited account of my annual trip to Europe, Tuxedo tried to jump down from her lap, staggered a little, then collapsed at my feet. His long, thick coat had always made him look bigger than he really was, but he'd grown leaner with age. When I picked him up, however, I realized he'd lost a huge amount of weight in the few weeks I'd been away.

I cradled him in my arms like a baby, something he rarely tolerated from anyone but my mother. Now he lay there passively, too lethargic to object. I could feel every vertebra in his spine poking sharply beneath his skin.

"Well, his appetite's been a bit off," my mother confirmed, when I asked if she'd noticed anything amiss. "And now that you mention it, he seems to be drinking a lot more than usual."

I didn't like the sound of that. Tux had never been sick a day in his life, but there was no question he was very ill now.

"It could be that he missed you," my mother suggested hopefully. We both feared there was more to it, though, and I made an appointment at our animal clinic for that afternoon.

The diagnosis was kidney failure. "The kindest thing would be to put him down," the vet told me, concluding his examination. "He's eighteen years old and done well to last this long, but I'm afraid he's finally used up his nine lives. I'll hook him up to an IV if that's what you want, but you won't be doing yourself or him any favors. He's dying, Mrs. Wexley."

I stroked Tuxie's still-luxurious fur. "How can he have gone downhill so quickly?"

"Cats tend to do that. They compensate until they can't manage anymore."

Barely in check from having so recently left Marco, my emotions bubbled over. "He's part of the family," I whimpered, the tears springing to my eyes.

"Yes. For those of us who love our pets, they always are and letting them go is always painful." He stroked Tuxie's handsome head, his touch full of compassion. "Would it help if you took him home and gave everyone a chance to say goodbye, then brought him back later on?"

"Should I? Is it fair to him? Is he suffering?"

He shook his head. "The old gentleman's hardly aware anymore."

I could see that for myself. When I'd first put him in a cardboard box and taken him to the car to bring him to the clinic, he'd roused himself enough to voice his objections, and tried to push open the lid. Now, he didn't have the strength to stand up.

I wrapped him in his blanket and kept him on the seat beside me during the drive home. My mother met me at the door, and simply held out her arms to take him. She carried him to her rocking chair on the porch where the two of them had sat for so many hours these last four summers and settled him on her lap. He died there about an hour later.

We buried him in the garden, under the pear tree.

A week later, I came home from grocery shopping and found my sweet mother dead in that same chair. Her hands rested peacefully on its arms, and her eyes gazed unseeingly on the place where Tuxie lay. A massive heart attack, the autopsy revealed.

I was racked with grief and guilt. How could I have let this happen? Was it because I'd been too wrapped up in my own life to pay proper attention to hers? Or had she, like Tuxedo, hidden the signs and slipped away when no one was looking?

Our doctor tried to comfort me. "She never saw it

coming, Anna. It struck suddenly and without warning. She felt no pain."

He had it all backward, though. She was seventy-one and should've had many more years with us, but she'd lost her faithful companion, and the pain had broken her heart. I understood how that could be.

Grace came home for the funeral and took a week's leave of absence from her school to stay with us. "Maybe you should consider selling this place and moving into a smaller house, Mother, especially with Daddy being away so much," she suggested before leaving again.

But we'd lived there almost thirty years, and the house held too many precious memories I wasn't ready to give up. Nor did it seem a good idea to make such a major decision while we were in mourning. "Perhaps when things settle down a bit," I said. "It's been a rough month."

But the worst wasn't quite over. Two days before Thanksgiving, Peggy's son phoned to tell us she'd died in hospital of a brain aneurysm. She would've turned eighty-one December first. I had never needed Marco more and lived for his next letter.

Firenze
December 15, 1968
Anna, *tesoro mio,*
How I wish I could be with you at this time. Even more, I wish I could take your sorrow and carry it on my own shoulders. Why so much loss of loved ones in such a brief span, you wonder, and I am reminded that we have a saying here in Italy that death never travels alone. It prefers to arrive in threes.

If that is indeed so, you've had your share for several years to come.

Please do not worry about my leg. I promise you, it's as good as new. I have no special plans for Christmas this year. Claudia is nineteen now and well understands the situation between her mother and me, so I see no use in pretending we are all one big, happy Italian family wallowing in sentimentality and olive oil. Rudolfo and his wife have invited me to join them on Christmas Eve, and I shall meet with my mother and sisters for dinner on Christmas Day. Apart from that, I intend to relax with a bottle of good wine, a good book and memories of you.

Already, I'm looking ahead to August and thinking of places I might take you, after we've been to Cambridge. We've "done" England to the point where there's little else to see, and you opened my eyes to all kinds of possibilities when you spirited me away to St. Moritz last summer. How would you like to see Ireland, for a change, or France? The past months have been unkind to you, my dearest love, but much joy still lies ahead.

I shall miss speaking to you on the twenty-fifth, but as you'll be visiting Brian's parents, it's hardly appropriate for me to phone you there. Nor will I send you roses. Instead I enclose with this letter a token of my deep and abiding love for you.

Safe journey to Florida and home again, my darling. Know that, as always, I'll be thinking of you and missing you.

Marco

I understood now why he'd chosen such a sturdy envelope. Folded in tissue paper and tucked flat between the sheets of his letter, was a delicate gold heart pendant studded with a single diamond, suspended on a fine gold chain. Although we'd exchanged many gifts over the years—silk scarves and ties, books, prints, leather purses and belts—we'd studiously avoided anything too extravagantly personal, so as not to invite awkward questions.

Certainly we'd never given jewelry, and that he broke with tradition now meant everything to me. The pendant represented the wedding ring he'd never been able to put on my finger. I hung it around my neck right away and have never taken it off since.

Grace sent a very special gift that Christmas, too. In addition to a lovely quilted satin bathrobe for me and a new pair of binoculars for her father, she told us she'd be leaving her current teaching position in June and taking a job closer to home. Apparently, when she was here for her grandmother's funeral, she'd run into an old high school friend, a certain good-looking young man she'd had a crush on since her sophomore year, and they had, as she put it, "reconnected."

At that, Carly, who's been mopping her eyes constantly for several minutes, breaks into a smile. "My father?"

"That's right, precious. They announced their engagement when she came home for Easter, with the wedding set for the following June. Plenty of time for us to plan a grand affair, I thought, almost as giddy with happiness as she was. My one regret was that Marco's name couldn't be included on the guest list.

"'Well, I don't see why not,' your grandpa remarked,

when I said as much. 'Who's going to question it? Weddings have always been a time for friends you haven't seen in years to get together and celebrate.'

"Was it possible? I asked myself. Dared we risk it? Or would people take one look at us and leap to the conclusion Marco and I were far more than just friends?"

CHAPTER FIFTEEN

MARCO AND I sat in the garden of the whitewashed cottage where we'd taken a room for the night, with Ireland spread around us in every shade of green under the sun. Poppies grew in the cracks of the old stone wall. Somewhere in the distance, a cuckoo called. Closer at hand, robins and chaffinches flew back and forth to a feeder hanging in a rowan tree.

"How is it that, despite the miles between us, our lives always seem to follow similar paths?" I said. "First, Grace gets engaged and then, within a month, Claudia, too."

"I take it as a sign that fate meant for us to be together," Marco said, idly playing with my hair.

"I wish you'd reconsider and come to the wedding, Marco."

"I don't belong there, my love. This is a special event between a mother and her daughter."

Not all that special, at least for Grace and me. We might not be at loggerheads anymore, but I likened my relationship with her to walking on thin ice. She had definite ideas about how her wedding should be, and I knew better than to try imposing my views.

"What if it had been Steven who was getting married?" I asked Marco.

He laughed. "I'd still have to say no. He resembled me too closely. People would have been sure to notice and wonder."

"But Grace isn't—"

"No, Anna," he said flatly. "I have never been ashamed of loving you. Don't ask me to start hiding it now and pretend to your relatives that I'm nothing but an old friend. It's more than I can do."

He was right, of course. Except for my brief stay in Florence the previous summer, we'd managed to keep our affair secret because we'd confined ourselves to neutral territory. Grace's wedding day wasn't the time to go public. But the last year had made me very conscious of the frailty of human life, and reuniting with him in London a week ago hadn't exactly reassured me. His hair had turned completely silver since I'd last seen him, and he walked with a slight limp now. More than that, I noticed a tiredness in him that was new.

It was particularly evident the next night. We'd made reservations at an eighteenth-century castle-turned-hotel, a hundred miles to the north. Marco had always been a man of boundless energy, but after we'd checked in and he'd climbed the stairs to our tower suite, his face was gray with fatigue. The room faced west with a sweeping view of the dramatic coastline, and normally he'd have gone straight to the window to photograph the sunset. That afternoon, he lowered himself to the settee beside the hearth where a peat fire burned to ward off the evening chill, and gingerly massaged his leg.

Concerned, because it wasn't the first time I'd seen him do this, I said, "You told me your leg had healed perfectly."

"Stiffened up a bit from sitting too long in the car, that's all," he answered brusquely. "It happens sometimes."

I was tempted to point out that it appeared to happen rather more often than "sometimes," but he clearly didn't want to discuss the subject, so I poured us each a glass of sherry from the decanter on the dresser and joined him by the fire.

The hotel owners had provided every modern comfort for their guests, without sacrificing the antiquity and ambience of the castle. The room was charming with its four-poster bed and glass-domed oil lamps artfully converted to electricity. Very atmospheric and romantic.

And two steep, punishing flights of stairs removed from the main floor. "I'm kind of beat myself," I said, with a clumsy attempt at subtlety. "Do you suppose we could have dinner served up here?"

Not fooled for a minute, he caught my hand and kissed my fingers. "Am I growing old and bad-tempered, *carissima?*"

"No. You're not as young as you once were, that's all, and neither am I. And this is such a lovely room, it's a shame not to enjoy it."

But he wouldn't hear of it, and insisted we dress for dinner in the dining hall. "You look like a queen, Anna. Will you be ashamed to be seen with a mere working man like me?" he murmured, coming up behind me and dropping a kiss at the side of my neck as I stood before the mirror, putting the final touches to my hair.

"Not if you straighten your tie," I teased, shifting in his arms and kissing him back.

As it turned out, we enjoyed ourselves so much that evening, I persuaded him to extend our stay by another two days. We'd been on the move constantly since leaving Cambridge, never staying more than a night in any one place, and it occurred to me this contributed to his fatigue.

The next morning, we toured the wine cellar and took morning coffee in the library. Then, after an early lunch, we joined one of the couples from the night before and played a round on the hotel's par three golf course, returning to our suite in the late afternoon, soaked to the skin in the cloudburst that hit as we approached the last hole.

Our bathroom was huge, the tub a restored cast-iron behemoth deep enough to drown in, the hot water supply apparently endless. We'd had our share of escapades in bathtubs over the years, but this one presented a whole new range of possibilities, and love in the afternoon had always ranked high on our list of favorite pastimes.

A pity we weren't as agile as we'd once been, but there was much to be said for the slow, sweet passion of middle age, the tender exploration of bodies familiar yet still exciting. Considering we were well past the first flush of youth, we managed to please each other very well.

Loath to leave it after we'd made love, we drained the tub and refilled it, adding a handful of herbal bath crystals to the water. "I shall remember this day when January comes and even Firenze is cold and damp," Marco said, stroking my stomach as I reclined against him while the rain beat against the windowpanes and the peat fire glowed through the open door to the bedroom.

I sighed, the specter of another year without him looming too close. "If it was up to me, we'd never be apart again. I'd stay with you forever."

His hand slid up and stilled, cupping my breast possessively. "Don't tempt me, *carissima*. We both know the price you'd have to pay."

"I'd do it anyway if you asked me to."

"It wouldn't be as easy as you imagine, to throw over the life you've built for yourself in America, and the moral compass by which you've lived it."

"I've been your mistress for sixteen years, Marco. A lot of people would say I don't have a moral compass worth mentioning."

Distressed, he muttered, "Don't say that. You are my wife in every way that counts."

"You're right," I said, regretting my hasty words. "It's more that I feel we're such gypsies, forever wandering the world, looking for a place to live. Do you think we could buy a little house or cottage and stay there instead of always being on the move?"

"Are you tired of traveling, my love?"

"Not that, so much as wishing we had a place we could call home. Something permanent, with an address and things in it that we've chosen together. A place that's all ours."

"The idea has merit, I suppose."

I heard the reservation in his voice. "But you're not in favor of it?"

"I question how practical it is, Anna. A house standing empty eleven months of the year…"

"Why should it have to?" I cried, our self-imposed exile from each other suddenly more than I could bear. "Our children are adults, on the verge of marriage. You live alone and so, to a very large extent, do I. Haven't we reached a point where the legalities of our relationship are mere technicalities? Is anyone really going to care if we live together as husband and wife without documentation to make it official?"

"Yes," he said. "*You* will care. You will care what your daughter thinks of you for leaving her father to fend for himself. You will care that I cannot take you to meet my mother and sisters, or introduce you as my wife in certain circles. And very soon, you'll ask yourself if I'm worth the pain I'm causing you. And then, *I* will care, because I would rather have you to myself for one month of the year than risk losing you altogether."

My frustration died as swiftly as it had arisen. "You're right again. But we miss so much—all the big days, the important anniversaries, when we should be together and aren't."

"Not so," he said, scooping me back so that I was plastered against his chest and he could nuzzle the curve of my shoulder. "When we're together, those *are* the big days. The memories they bring are what keep us connected, no matter the miles between us."

I TRIED to remember his words on Grace's wedding day, as I sat at the reception, looking very much the mother of the bride in pale blue crepe and feeling equally blue inside when the best man raised his glass in a toast to absent loved ones. Grace and Taylor were so deeply, joyously in love, but with my mother and father gone, Peggy, too, and memories of my precious Steven suddenly very close to the surface, I felt utterly alone.

A week later, Marco walked Claudia down the aisle and within the year became a grandfather. She gave birth to a son in April 1973. For a few short weeks, Brian and I also looked forward to welcoming a grandchild, but Grace miscarried in her second month and was so distraught that I canceled my trip to Europe that year, in order to be with her.

"My darling Anna, of course I understand," Marco said when I phoned with the news.

"Will you still go to Cambridge and leave flowers for him, and tell him we miss him?"

"Yes," he assured me, recognizing that although my place was with my daughter at this difficult time, a part of me yearned to be with my son, too. In the twenty-one years since we'd lost him, I'd never once missed visiting his grave on the anniversary of his death. "I will be there for both of us."

"It's a good thing we didn't follow up on the idea of buying a house," I said.

"It could still happen, my love. There's no guessing what the future might bring."

"We're getting too old to bank on the future, Marco."

"We will never be too old," he said. "You feel like that right now because you're sad for Grace, but trust me when I tell you she'll have better luck the next time, and you'll realize then what I've recently learned, which is that grandchildren are one of our greatest gifts and the joy of our old age."

WHEN WE MET NEXT, in 1974, Marco had a surprise for me. After Cambridge, he whisked me across the Channel and back to St. Moritz, not to the hotel we'd stayed in before, but to a small private chalet on the lake.

"It's ours," he said, when I asked. "I have leased it every August for as many years as we want it."

It proved the perfect solution for us in that we had all the pleasure and privilege of our own private hideaway, with none of the responsibility for its upkeep the rest of the year. We even had a deep storage area under the stairs where we could keep a few personal items—books, framed photographs, crystal wineglasses, and such—to lend the place the touch of a real home when we were in residence.

We spent the month making up for the twenty-four we'd been apart, sleeping late, lazing on the sunny deck, spoiling each other with little gifts and making love whenever the mood took us without worrying about check-out times or train schedules.

Leaving him was never easy, but having a place to come back to helped a little when our last day together arrived.

SADLY, Grace miscarried twice more over the next year and a half. We'd achieved a better understanding since she married Taylor. The love of a good man blunted her sharp edges and let her finally forgive me for not living up to her idea of what the mother of a teenager should be, and we were never closer than when we came together as women grieving for their lost children. It was the one instance she never accused me of not understanding, because she knew very well that I did.

Discouraged after her third pregnancy failed, she abandoned motherhood and decided to concentrate on her career instead. In 1975, she became principal of the primary school she and Steven had once attended, investing in her charges all the love and attention she'd hoped to lavish on her own child.

That same year, Marco's mother died. She was eighty-seven.

Although he mourned her loss, he recognized that she'd had a long, full life, and took comfort in Oreste, his grandson, whom he adored and with whom he enjoyed the closeness he'd been denied with Claudia when she was young.

I envied him Oreste. I'd seen photographs of the boy and he was beautiful, a miniature of Marco as I imagined he must have looked at that age, with big dark eyes, silky black hair and a winning smile. "We'll share him," Marco used to say, and I loved him for it, but my heart ached for Grace and Taylor who'd so wanted a family of their own.

Then, when they'd put aside all hopes of ever becoming parents, Grace got pregnant again at thirty-eight and, under the care of an excellent obstetrician, gave birth in 1980 to my precious Carly. At last, I had a grandbaby to rock on the porch, in the same chair where my mother once sat and rocked my babies.

Ever a loving and patient father, Brian was, just as I'd expected, a doting grandfather. In retirement, the brilliant mathematician and man of the sea developed an aptitude with tools and started working with his hands. He built charming, whimsical birdhouses and an endless succession of toys for his granddaughter.

I smile as I remind Carly of them. "A miniature wheelbarrow, a wishing well, a cradle for your dolls and a mother duck and four duckling, all painted yellow and mounted on bright red wheels. You towed them behind you everywhere you went when you first learned to walk."

Carly's eyes grow soft with affection. "I remember. I loved them all, but that was my favorite. They were happy days, weren't they, Gran?"

"Indeed they were. For a few years, life was as close to perfect as I could ask. Marco and I had arrived at an acceptance of our circumstances and learned to make the best of them. Your parents' happiness was complete. Your grandfather felt contented. And I was in my element shopping for a little girl again. Dressing you up, painting your toenails pink, curling your hair, sewing clothes for your dolls, afforded me such pleasure...."

But experience had taught me that although tragedy might lie low for a while, it could strike without warning and change everything in the blink of an eye. And it did, in 1983, when Genevieve died after a short and vicious battle with breast cancer. During the final weeks of her illness, we were together more than we had been in the preceding twenty-five years. Treatment and disease had ravaged her body, stripping away its flesh and robbing her of her once-glorious red hair, but the light in her eyes never dimmed and she fought that evil predator to her last breath. She was sixty-two.

Seven years later, Giulia fell victim to cancer, also.

"I grieve not for her death," Marco said that summer, "but for the life she never had the courage to live. She took no joy in motherhood and barely knew her grandson. I hope I leave a more lasting legacy when I go."

"I don't want to hear you talk like that," I reproached him. The years had been kind to both of us, but they were slipping by too fast. I was sixty-nine, he, seventy-three, and although our love for each other, and indeed our desire, burned strong as ever, age was making its presence felt.

Too rich or late a dinner produced heartburn. The espresso coffee he'd taught me to enjoy caused insomnia. Too much liquid of any kind after eight o'clock in the evening meant two or three trips to the bathroom during the night. He now walked with a cane. I couldn't wear heels anymore. But as long as we had our Augusts together, and in-between times, the phone to connect us and photographs to remind us of summers past, we were, if not completely satisfied, at least content.

Of course I knew it all had to come to an end eventually, but I wasn't going to waste however much time remained fretting about it.

One year, on the eve of my departure, we took a last walk by the lake. The moon rode high, illuminating the snow on the highest peaks and flinging a silvery glow on the water. Although our imminent leave-taking always cast a shadow on those final few hours together, he seemed unusually preoccupied that night. "You're very quiet, sweetheart," I said.

"Because," he told me, "I'm trying to gather the courage to say something."

Having no clue what he was talking about, I almost laughed. "Since when have you lacked courage? Spit it out, whatever it is."

"*Va bene,* then. All right." He stopped and turned me to face him. "I've come close to asking you this many times, but it would have been unfair to make you choose between me and your family. But now they no longer need you as they once did, and I need you desperately. So, Anna my dearest love, will you marry me?"

CHAPTER SIXTEEN

I STARED AT HIM, completely at a loss. For years, I'd longed to hear those words. And now that he was in a position to make it possible, legally and before God, I had to refuse him, because how could I leave Brian at his age? How could I walk away from Carly, the light of my life?

I couldn't!

I pressed my fingers to my mouth, beating them lightly against my lips in a futile effort to stop the tears that threatened to choke me at fate's unkind trick.

He knew without my having to say a word what my answer would be. "It's all right, *amore mio*. I really didn't expect you to say yes."

"Then why did you ask me?"

"Because marriage is what I've most wanted to offer you, but I haven't been free to do so until now."

"I'd accept in a heartbeat if I could, and more often than I can count I would've said yes and let the rest of the world go hang itself. But you were right, that summer in Ireland, when you said I'd never be able to sever my ties to home. It's not that I don't love you or want to be with you. I do! But the timing is all wrong."

He stroked my face lovingly. "It always has been, Anna. Fate has been against us from the start."

I leaned against him and kissed him. "Maybe not. Maybe the reason we're still so much in love is that we're together too briefly to get tired of each other."

That wasn't really the reason, and we both knew it. If all we'd felt was infatuation, we'd have lost touch long ago. But our love had overcome every obstacle thrown in its way.

That night, we made love with a passion we hadn't experienced in years. Almost, I thought in the warm, sleepy aftermath, as if we might never have the chance again.

WE NEVER DID, not in St. Moritz. The next year, after visiting Steven's grave, we spent August in Florence, back where our romance had begun. Widowed over a year by then, Marco could be seen with me in public without fear of incurring censure.

I met Oreste, a charming, handsome, intelligent young man. What endeared him to me was his tender, respectful concern for Marco, and his unquestioning acceptance of my place in Marco's life. I suspect he was very well acquainted with the kind of marriage his grandfather had endured.

"I'll be the chauffeur, *Nonno*," he always insisted on the occasions the three of us went out together. "You and Anna sit together in the backseat and hold hands."

When the month was up, he drove us to the airport and kissed me on both cheeks. "Until next year, Anna. Be very good to yourself in the meantime," he said, then waited in the car so Marco and I could spend a few minutes alone.

"He's a remarkable young man, and so much like you, it's uncanny," I said, watching him stride away. "He even walks like you—or at least, the way you did when you were younger."

But Marco's attention was on me, and for the first time in all our goodbyes, he had tears in his eyes. "Every year, it grows harder for me to let you go," he said, his voice husky. "This year is the most difficult of all."

He didn't need to elaborate. We never talked about it, but we were both aware that time was no longer on our side. We didn't have the stamina of our youth. Our emotions lay closer to the surface, more easily touched. We weren't as resilient as we'd been.

"I'll be back, I promise," I said, around the lump in my throat.

"And I was," I tell Carly, "for the next three years."

"Then what happened?"

"Your grandpa hadn't been himself. I couldn't quite put my finger on the trouble, but something wasn't right.

"'I'm fine,' he insisted when I questioned him. 'A bit tired at the end of the day, but that's normal at my age.'

"I couldn't argue with that. He was seventy-eight, after all. But he'd always had so much energy. As recently as the summer just past, he'd enjoyed gardening, taking his daily two-mile walk, playing bridge. But with the shorter days of winter, he grew increasingly lethargic, caught cold more easily, was often feverish and suffered frequent headaches.

"'What else do you expect?' he snapped, when I dared to comment. 'Everybody's coughing and sneezing.'

"'I'm not, Brian.'

"'You're a woman,' he said, showing a marked lack of logic for a mathematician. 'Women don't get sick. They just suffer in silence.'

"'They also worry about their husbands,' I told him, 'so whether or not you like it, I'm making an appointment for you to see the doctor.'"

Carly nods. "I was almost thirteen then, and I remember Mom being really worried about him, too. What did the doctor say?"

"That your grandpa had mononucleosis."

"Not the best diagnosis for a man his age, but it could've been a lot worse," she comments. "You must've been relieved, Gran."

"Oh, I was, Carly." I don't add that I'd been terribly afraid he'd contracted AIDS. To do so would betray his secret. "He was ordered to take it easy for a month, then he'd be a hundred percent again."

"But he wasn't, was he?"

"No. He continued to lose weight and by Christmas he'd dropped to a hundred and sixty pounds, twenty less than usual and down thirty from when he was in his prime. Further tests in the new year, including the biopsy of a swollen gland in his neck, brought in a different diagnosis. He had non-Hodgkin's lymphoma and was immediately started on an aggressive course of treatment."

"I remember," Carly whispers.

"I didn't go to Europe that August. I buried my husband, instead. I had never loved him more than I did during those arduous months when he fought so hard to overcome the odds."

"They were stacked against him from the outset," Carly says sadly. "Chemotherapy often isn't very effective in people his age."

"So we learned after the fact."

"It must've been hard on you, too, Gran. Physically and emotionally."

"It was," I admit. "Although I wrestled with the decision over the next winter, by spring I faced the fact that I could no longer keep up the house I'd lived in for so long. But I couldn't face strangers living there, either, so I handed it over to your parents and moved into an apartment not far away."

"Why didn't you live with us? We had plenty of room."

"There was never any question of that. Your mother and I had made our peace years ago, but it was a fragile truce. We can take each other in small doses."

"I guess I've always known that, but I've never understood why."

"She disapproved of how I lived my life and would've run it for me if she could, but I cherished my independence too much to let her."

"Why didn't you spend the summer with Marco? There was nothing to keep you in Rhode Island anymore and the change would've done you good."

"Setting up my new home took more out of me than I expected, and I didn't have the energy to face the long trip to Europe. We made do with phone calls instead, running up huge long-distance charges every month. Fortunately, money had never been a problem for either of us."

"When did you see him again?"

"Not until 1996 when I flew straight to Florence. He and Oreste met me and drove me to a sixteenth-century villa in the country that catered to guests."

It had creamy-yellow walls and a red tile roof and was surrounded by olive groves, orchards and fields of wildflowers.

In the two years since Marco and I had been together,

time had left its mark on both of us. I was seventy-six and he was eighty. He walked with difficulty, despite his cane. My knees creaked when I sat down. Stairs made me breathless. We both needed glasses—one pair for reading, another for distance.

No longer able to explore as we once used to, we were content to spend our days strolling hand in hand through the paths in the gardens, or resting in the shade of the terrace and talking about everything under the sun. Peaceful, golden days, full of laughter and sometimes a few tears, but always, always, full of love.

We enjoyed *caffé latte* in the morning and a glass of wine at sunset. We dined in the garden on simple Tuscan food. Risotto and steamed fish or roasted chicken flavored with herbs from the garden. And when the moon rose over the olive groves, we went upstairs to our airy, spacious room with its frescoed walls and climbed into our bed and held each other, and prayed for another day, another night, together.

Too soon, I had to leave, and although neither of us admitted it, we both accepted that I wouldn't be back to visit him and that we'd never again make the pilgrimage to Cambridge. But we knew, too, that nothing—not time, distance, life or death—would ever touch our love. He was my heart, and I was his.

Two years later, he suffered a stroke that left him with slight paralysis on his right side. Stairs were a problem, and unable to manage well in his loft apartment, he went to live with Oreste, who by then owned a vineyard about an hour southwest of Florence, in Chianti wine country.

My health declined also, which was why I moved into the retirement home where I had access to round-the-clock nursing if I needed it. Grace and Taylor were a thirty-minute drive away, and Carly could be there in forty-five. I responded well to medication. With care, the doctors told me, I could live another ten years. Not that I believed them for a minute.

"You'll be around until you're a hundred, if I have my way," Carly says, her voice wobbling with yet more tears. "You must take really good care of yourself, Gran, and not overdo it."

I shake my head and smile. Neither of us is fooled into believing I'm going to last that long. "You were always my greatest champion, precious, but old hearts don't keep ticking forever, and mine's fast wearing out, which is why I want to spend however many days I have left with Marco. I want to sit beside him again and hold his hand as we watch the sun set over the Tuscan hills. I want to experience the joy that being with him has always brought me. Before I die, I want one last summer in Italy with the great love of my life."

She nods tearfully.

"That's why I called on you, my beautiful granddaughter and greatest ally, because if anyone could make it happen, you could and you would. I'm so glad you're here with me and have listened so patiently to my story."

"I'm glad, too. I've never met Marco but I feel I know him, and I have a much better understanding now about your relationship." She hesitates briefly. "I have a question, Gran."

"Then ask it."

"Did you really love Grandpa, or did you tell me that to make me feel better?"

"Oh, darling, I loved him dearly, and he loved me."

"Did you ever meet the other woman—Grandpa's, I mean?"

"Never," I say, relieved that I'd managed to cover up the truth well enough that she hadn't guessed how it really played out, and had leapt to the conventional conclusion. "We kept our separate lives separate. It seemed the best thing to do."

"Didn't it bother you, living a lie all those years?"

Oh, yes! I'd been terrified Brian's secret would leak out. Not that I could tell Carly that.

"I'd have preferred not to, but the truth would have hurt too many people, and I don't believe there's anything noble about inflicting needless suffering. Your grandfather and I had an understanding that allowed us both to be happy." I venture a glance at her. "Are you very disappointed in me, precious?"

She sighs almost dreamily and shakes her head. "Actually I think it's all rather romantic. I can hardly wait to meet this charismatic man who swept my very proper Gran off her feet and into his bed. He must really be something."

"Oh, he was when he was young," I say with a laugh. "To me, he always will be."

ORESTE IS WAITING when we arrive in Florence. "You look wonderful, Anna," he exclaims, enfolding me in a hug.

He looks wonderful, too. The young man I'd last seen seven years ago has come into his own. At twenty-seven, with an easy self-assurance and looks any movie star would be happy to own, he is, as my granddaughter would say, really something. And she notices.

"Hi," she says, self-consciously pushing a wayward strand of hair into place as I introduce her. "I've heard a lot about you."

He fixes her in his melting brown gaze. "And I have heard almost nothing about you. What a good thing we'll have the chance to become acquainted while you're here. Let me take those baggage-claim slips and collect your luggage. Your grandmother should not be standing so long."

Oh, the Latin charm!

Uncommonly pink and flustered, Carly steers me to a bank of chairs. "Wow!" she breathes, her eyes tracking him as he effortlessly hauls the first of our heavy suitcases off the luggage carousel.

I understand the effect he has on her. Marco beguiled me that easily, too, and I never recovered. No question in my mind but that in Oreste's case, the apple hasn't fallen far from the grandfatherly tree. Why he isn't already married or spoken for baffles me.

"Plenty of women chase after him," Marco told me once when I questioned him on this. "But he's choosy, like me. Not just any woman will do."

Within the hour, we're on our way, soon leaving the city behind and heading for Marco's beloved Tuscan hills. Heat shimmers in the still air and creates mirages on the road surface, but air-conditioning keeps us pleasantly cool in the car.

We pass by Greve, turn off the main highway a few miles north of Siena and follow a road winding between hectares of vineyards at the end of which stands his home. Set in several acres of gardens, the villa rises from the landscape, its white stucco walls dazzling in the sun. I'm sure there are other features meriting recognition, but at this moment I'm too filled with the familiar stirring of anticipation to notice anything else. Soon I will be with Marco again.

Sensing my impatience, Oreste ushers us inside and through a wide hall to a terrace at the rear, near the swimming pool. And there he is, my darling, my love, rising from his chair to greet me. His cane is close by, but he stands unaided, not as tall as he used to be and no longer powerfully built, but still the man I fell in love with, more years ago than I care to count. My old heart kicks up a pace, and I cover the distance between us with a spring in my step that I hadn't managed in years.

His good arm closes around me and we cling to each other, our tears running together. "*Ciao,* my beautiful girl," he whispers. "Welcome home."

If I died at this moment, I would leave the world a happy woman. But God hasn't finished with me or Marco yet. Taking charge, Oreste introduces Carly and draws forward chairs. He serves cold drinks from a trolley and we sit, making small talk to ease the slight awkwardness of strangers meeting for the first time. Eventually, though, he takes Carly inside and leaves us alone.

Marco reaches across the small space separating us and clasps my hand. We smile, a wonderful serenity settling over us. Talking can wait. Once again, we've been granted a tomorrow.

We eat dinner early that evening, a light, delicious meal prepared by a housekeeper who comes in daily. Shortly after, Marco and I retire to his main-floor suite. He has a sitting room that opens to a vine-shaded pergola, a bedroom and a bathroom equipped for his safety because, as Oreste confided to me in an aside during the meal, his grandfather remains fiercely independent despite the disability brought on by his stroke. "He won't give in to it," he murmured.

"His philosophy is that the day he lets it get the better of him, he might as well take to his bed and stay there."

Yes, that's the man I know.

My suitcases, I discover, have been unpacked in Marco's dressing room and my clothes hung next to his. Smiling, I say, "I wondered where I'd be sleeping."

"With me, of course," he murmurs, looping his hand around my waist. "Where else, *carissima?*"

I am eighty-three and he'll be eighty-seven in another three months, but he hasn't forgotten how to make my heart soar.

WE SPEND a leisurely two weeks, needing nothing but each other's company to be happy. The days of romping between the sheets or hijinks in a bathtub are long gone. We still make love all the time, but differently. With a touch, a glance, a smile, a kiss. The years have taken our once-effervescent passion and rendered it down to a sweet, still concentrate, eternal as the sunrise.

Carly keeps a sternly professional eye on us, but finds opportunities to enjoy herself with Oreste. Often, while we nap, he takes her sightseeing or shows her his estate, but they also spend many an hour swimming or lying stretched out by the pool, sharing conversations we can't hear and laughing quietly together.

Then Marco and I exchange hopeful glances. "Do you suppose?" I say, resorting to the verbal shorthand of a couple who are intimately familiar each other's thoughts.

"Parafulmine?" The laughter creases around his eyes deepen. "It's been known to happen."

"Wouldn't it be wonderful?"

"We mustn't push."

"No."

I experience a great sense of peace during these un-hurried days.

A readiness, you might call it. But life has still another surprise in store.

One particularly beautiful night, so full of stars they almost cast a shadow, Marco and I sit on the love seat under the pergola. "What's going on in that head of yours?" I ask, after a silence lasting ten minutes or more.

"I'm working up the nerve to ask you a question," he says, the ghost of a smile hovering around his mouth. "One I've asked you twice before. I'm hoping the third time will be the charm, as the English say. Will you marry me, Anna?"

Is he teasing me? Confused?

But his gaze is focused on me with absolute clarity and attention, and the lighthearted reply I'm about to utter dies on my lips.

I count all the things I love about him. His gentleness, his masculinity. The way he looks at me, touches me, knows what I'm thinking almost before I do.

I remember when our hunger for each other could never be satisfied, and the quiet interludes when simply being in the same room was all we needed to make an afternoon or evening perfect.

I remember how we'd always been able to talk, about anything and everything, and the contented silence between us when words weren't necessary.

And I know he's waited long enough for me to give him the answer we've both yearned to hear.

"Yes, Marco, my love," I say. "I will marry you."

CHAPTER SEVENTEEN

"IT CAN'T BE DONE," Carly said when she heard. "This is Italy and my grandmother's an American citizen."

"It can be done," Oreste insisted. "There is always a way, and we will uncover it. We will make this happen."

She didn't see how. Quite apart from the legal requirements, there was her mother to consider. Throwing a wedding into an already volatile mix would take some doing. Yet seeing the way her grandmother and Marco looked at each other, Carly knew she *had* to.

"They're worse than a pair of teenagers," she said.

Oreste smiled and brought her hand to his lips. "Love has nothing to do with age, *mia bella.*"

His touch sent the heat surging to her face.

Last night, he'd kissed her on the mouth and she'd been shocked at her response, at the dizzying need he'd aroused in her. What was it about these Paretti men, that they could fell normally sane women with a single glance? "I suppose not," she mumbled, her common sense hanging by a thread.

"It would be as well to make arrangements quickly," he said now, looking past her to where the lovebirds sat in the shade of a sun umbrella.

She knew what he saw: two frail old people with not a lot of time left. "Where do we start?"

"With the most difficult, because I cannot help you with it. Anna has her passport, but she also must produce officially translated copies of her birth certificate and her husband's death certificate. Is there someone who can expedite this for you?"

"My father's a lawyer. He'll take care of it and ship everything to us by courier. What then?"

"We go to Florence and attend to the remaining formalities."

"How long is that likely to take?"

He shrugged, and she wished he hadn't. She had enough on her mind without her attention being drawn to his impressive width of shoulder. She knew from having seen him in bathing trunks how very nicely he was put together.

"Normally it is several weeks," he said, "but I anticipate an exception will be made in this case, in light of the advanced years of the betrothed."

He spoke excellent English, but sometimes, as now, his phrasing and vocabulary rang with a foreign and much-too-attractive cadence. Another distraction Carly didn't need. "We might as well get started, then," she said briskly. "I'll call my parents right away."

"Use the phone in my office." His tone said he understood it wasn't going to be an easy call. "You'll have greater privacy."

She half hoped no one would be home, but her mother answered on the first ring. "We spoke last night. Why are you calling again today?" she began, obviously recognizing not just Carly's voice, but the edge of tension in it. "Has something happened to Gran?"

"Kind of."

"What? Is it her heart?"

"You could say so, I suppose."

Her mother let out a gasp. "I warned you she never should've taken that trip! But would anyone listen to me? Oh, no! You and your father and that damn-fool doctor she's so fond of were all so convinced you knew better."

"It's not quite what you think, Mom," Carly cut in, any hope of an easy way to break the news fast disappearing.

"Exactly what is it, then? Stop dancing around the subject, Carly, and tell me what's happened before my heart gives out, too."

"She's getting married."

She held her breath, waiting for the disbelieving hoot of laughter or outrage she was sure would greet her announcement. Instead a full ten seconds of silence ticked by before a quiet groan floated across the miles and her mother said dully, "It's that man again, isn't it? That Marco Paretti. He's still pulling the strings. I should've seen this coming a mile away."

Surprised, Carly blurted out, "You know about him?"

"Yes, I know about him." Her mother's scathing tone could have cut glass. "He and your grandfather met during the war and became friends, but he's had his eye on your grandmother for years, ever since we lived in England and went to Switzerland one Christmas."

Not *exactly* how it really began, but too close to the truth for Carly to refute. "That was ages ago, Mom. A lot's happened since then."

"Maybe, but it doesn't change the past. My father really loved my mother, and that man tried to come between them."

"She loved Grandpa. You can't deny that. Remember how she nursed him when he was sick."

The snort of derision she'd expected earlier barreled down the phone then. "And lost her mind doing it if you ask me. How else do you account for this preposterous notion of getting married again at her age?"

"I don't think it's my place to judge. She's my grandmother and I want her to get the most out of however much time she has left. If marrying Marco will do it, I'm all for it."

"You're as hopeless a romantic as she is!"

You're probably right on both counts, Carly thought, her heart giving a little jump when she looked up and saw Oreste watching her from the doorway. "Try to be happy for her, Mom," she pleaded.

Her mother started to cry then, deep, rasping sobs that seemed to wrench the very breath from her lungs. "If she marries him, she'll never come home again."

"No, she won't. She'll live here with him and his son, in a beautiful house in a beautiful setting."

"She's already living in a beauti—"

"She's in a retirement home, Mom. Dress it up any way you choose, but it won't change the fact that she's living alone."

"I don't—it wasn't my…!"

"Carly?" Her father's voice came on the line. "What's going on? Why is your mother crying?"

Prepared for another round of scornful incredulity,

she repeated the news, but her father actually laughed. "Anna always did know how to surprise us. When's the wedding to be?"

"As soon as we can arrange it. I didn't say this to Mom, but we can't afford to delay, if you get my drift."

"I do," he said, sobering. "Keep us posted on the date, and we'll be there."

She heard a faint squawk from her mother. Realizing her father would have his hands full dealing with her, Carly quickly relayed the request for further documentation and ended the call.

"That went well," she said dryly as Oreste joined her at the desk. "You probably figured out that my mother's not exactly doing handsprings over taking on a stepfather at this stage of the game."

Although he didn't touch her, he stood close enough that she could see the faint stipple of beard along his jaw and feel his breath on her face. "She is in shock, *mia bella*. Let her get used to the idea, then call her again."

Carly backed away, afraid of how he made her feel— all jittery inside and unsure of herself, of what was happening between them. If she hadn't known better, she would've said she was falling in love.

It was out of the question, of course. She had her future all planned out, and no man was going to derail it, least of all one she'd just met and who didn't even live on the same continent. Long-distance romance might have suited her grandmother, but it wouldn't do for her. Yet whenever she thought about leaving Oreste, her insides fell in on themselves.

"It occurred to me," she said, sidling past him, "that it

might be nice if we put together a little reception for them—our grandparents, that is."

He treated her to another disarming shrug that so eloquently said *non problema! "Si."*

"We'll need flowers and a cake and champagne, and a photographer. Just because they're old shouldn't mean we don't make an occasion of it. And I don't believe my grandmother brought anything with her that would do as a wedding dress, so I'll need to take her shopping. You'll have to tell me where to go. And the ceremony or service or whatever, can it be held here?"

She was out of control. A babbling idiot. And it was all his fault. He silenced her simply and effectively by kissing her so thoroughly that her brain turned to mush. She went to shove him away, but her hands had a will of their own and wound around his neck, holding him fast. "Don't stop," she whispered against his mouth.

THE NECESSARY documentation arrived the following Monday. On the Tuesday, Oreste drove everyone to Florence. He didn't say as much, but Carly suspected he'd called in a few favors, given the speed and ease with which the remaining formalities were processed.

When he took them to lunch in the early afternoon, all sworn statements had been completed and the banns posted at the Town Hall. Barring any unforeseen problems, her grandmother and Marco would be married in two weeks, in a civil ceremony at the house, with Oreste and Carly as witnesses. If they decided to come, her parents would be the only other guests.

THAT EVENING, after Marco and Anna were in bed, Carly said, "I'd hoped we could take Gran shopping for a wedding outfit, but I doubt she's up for it. Today wore her out."

"Then you and I will go alone," Oreste said.

"I can't ask you to do that."

"Why not, Carly? What will it take for you to accept that I want to be with you and will use any excuse to make it happen?"

"How can you say that? You hardly know me."

"I know the things that matter." He cupped her face and wouldn't let her avoid his steady gaze. "I know that you are beautiful inside and out. I know, too, that you are afraid."

"Of *you?*" She tried to sound amused but succeeded only in sounding pitifully uncertain.

"Of yourself, Carly," he said. "Of falling in love. Why else do you shy away from me every time we're alone together?"

"I don't," she protested, even as she tried to squirm free. "And I'm not afraid."

His thumb danced over her mouth, more erotic than a kiss. "Then dare to tell me I'm wrong when I say you want me as much as I want you. That you, too, lie awake at night wondering if, when destiny brought you here, it had more in mind than reuniting our grandparents. Tell me, if you dare, that you're not starting to care for me as I have come to care for you."

She swallowed, willing herself to take up the challenge. And found that whatever else might be in her heart, lies had no place there. One little push, and she'd tumble so deeply into love with him she'd never be free again.

"Tell me," he persisted.

Pressing her fingertips to her temples, trying to clear her

mind, she said, "Stop it, Oreste! You must see that falling in love isn't an option for either of us."

"Why not?" he said again.

"Because it's…not convenient."

His laughter flowed over her. "Love doesn't concern itself with convenience, *carissima,* nor does it play by the rules others impose on it."

"It'll have to in our case. Too much else is going on."

But saying so didn't make it so. With each passing day, her defenses grew weaker. No matter how busy she was with the wedding, he was always with her, not merely as a physical presence she couldn't ignore, but more insidiously occupying her every waking moment and filling her dreams.

How do you know when love's real, Gran? she'd asked, a few short weeks ago.

When it consumes you, Anna had replied.

At the time, Carly hadn't believed it, but she did now. Her feelings for Oreste were eating her alive. He had become an essential part of her, the other half she hadn't even realized was missing. Life before him was of no consequence; a future without him, increasingly barren. Loving, being loved—when all was said and done, they were what really mattered.

AFTER SOME UNCERTAINTY, her father phoned to say he and her mother would be at the wedding, after all.

They arrived two days before, on the Thursday. In the morning, she put flowers in the guest room and conferred with the housekeeper about the evening meal, while Oreste took Marco to town for a haircut.

That was easy. But driving to the airport with Oreste that

afternoon was not. Her mother was attending very much under protest and Carly had cramps just thinking about what that might mean.

Sensing her apprehension as the first passengers began filtering through customs, Oreste tucked her hand more firmly in his and said, "Your mother is a civilized woman and will not create a scene."

"No, she won't, at least not in public, but she'll have plenty to say to me in private. I'll do my best to calm her down, but I don't mind telling you, I'm glad I'll have my father there for backup."

"You have me, too. Among the three of us, *amore,* we'll tame this formidable lady and have her eating out of our hands before nightfall."

The men Carly had dated in the past would have run in the other direction rather than risk getting caught in the cross fire of a family feud, but not Oreste. If possible, she fell just a little more deeply in love with him for that.

DINNER THAT EVENING was a strained affair, with Grace picking at her food and shooting covert glares across the table at Marco. He appeared either blessedly unaware of his future daughter-in-law's disapproval, or gallantly chose to ignore it. But Anna noticed, and Carly decided the sooner she and her mother had a heart-to-heart talk, the better, or the wedding would be an unmitigated disaster.

The grandparents ate sparingly as usual and retired early. Finding common ground, the way men who'd just met so often seemed able to do, Taylor and Oreste sipped grappa and talked easily about the law, wine, greenhouse gases and great art. When her mother announced that jet lag had caught up with her and she was going to her room, Carly seized the opportunity and went with her.

"So how do you feel, now that you've seen Marco and Gran together?" she began as soon as they were alone. "Aren't they sweet?"

Her mother gave a disparaging sniff. "That's hardly the word that comes to *my* mind."

"Oh, come on, Mom, lighten up! They're old and in failing health, but they're determined to live until they die, which is more than can be said for a lot of people their age. Can't you put your own feelings aside for once and just be happy for them?"

"I'm here, aren't I? What more do you want?"

Since verbal sparring was getting her precisely nowhere, Carly cut to the chase. "I want you to tell me why you've got such a hate-on for Marco. Because it's not so much that Gran's getting married again, it's that she's marrying *him,* isn't it?"

At first, she didn't think she'd get an answer. Her mother sat down at the dressing table, removed her wedding and engagements rings and regarded them broodingly.

Finally she swiveled to face Carly. "All right, then, I'll tell you, but I'm warning you now, it's not a pretty story." She took a deep breath. "I was fourteen and we had a school dance coming up with a twenties' theme. My mother had a flapper dress belonging to my grandmother, a gorgeous thing made of red satin and yards of silky black fringe that I used to stroke when I was little, loving the way it moved."

She took a tube of lotion, squeezed some onto her palm and massaged it into her hands, paying particular attention to her cuticles. "Mother had said I could borrow it and said she'd leave it out for me, but she forgot. I needed it for the next day, and when Peggy told me Mom had gone into the village to buy more milk, I went searching for it myself. It wasn't in her clothes closet, but she had a trunk under her bedroom window, very pretty with hand-painted flowers on the lid, where she kept mementoes and souvenirs, and I thought that might be where she kept the dress."

"Was it?"

"I have no idea. When I lifted the lid, the first thing I saw, right there where I couldn't miss it, was a stack of letters in blue envelopes with foreign stamps, tied together with ribbon. All except for one lying separate from the rest, with the envelope beside it, as if she'd been called away before she'd finished reading it and had hidden it there until later."

"And?"

"And I read it."

"Mom!"

"I know I shouldn't have, but I guess I'm not as high-minded as you, Carly. It was from Marco Paretti, and it was private and never meant for my eyes, but I didn't care. Not that there was anything particularly juicy in it. No lurid references to sex in cheap hotels. Mostly it was all about some project he was working on, and how he'd spent a Sunday with his daughter and taken her to a museum. He even sent his regards to my father."

"A perfectly innocent letter between friends, in other words."

"Hardly. Friends don't call each other 'beloved' and 'darling.' They don't carry on about how much they miss each other and can't wait until they meet again, and they certainly don't end a letter with 'I love you.'"

"Did you tell Gran what you'd done?"

"No. I put the letter back where I'd found it, shut the trunk and left the room. She came home soon after, we sat down to dinner and pretended everything was peachy. Except it wasn't, because my father wasn't there. He hardly ever came home for dinner and now I understood why, and I hated her for it. No wonder they slept in separate beds. I was surprised he could bear being in the same room with her."

Because you knew only half the story, Carly thought. "And you blamed Marco for all this?"

"Yes." She looked up and met Carly's gaze, her eyes bright with unshed tears. "He stole my mother from me when I was a teenager, and now he's stealing her again."

"Oh, Mom, you know that's not true. I've heard Gran say a hundred times that no matter how old you are, you'll always be her baby."

"According to her, maybe, but a child caught between parents trapped in a loveless marriage inevitably chooses sides, and I chose my father's. He's the one I could count on to be there when she took off every summer to be with Marco Paretti. So please don't ask me to put on a smiling face and dance at her wedding, because I can't and I won't. I'll be civil, but that's as far as I'm prepared to go."

Carly thought of a dozen different things she could have said in reply, but in the end, she was left with only one option. "Grandpa was there for you one month out of the year, Mom. The other eleven, he made token appearances as a father, and Gran was the one who picked up the slack. Did you never wonder why?"

"He was dedicated to his work."

"What if there was another reason—another *person* he wanted to be with more than he wanted to be with Gran?"

"I wouldn't blame him if he did. At least I never questioned that he loved me."

"Gran always loved you, too. She still does. If you asked her to walk away from Marco and go back to the States with you, she'd do it because your happiness matters more to her than her own or anyone else's. It's one reason she stayed with Grandpa instead of asking for a divorce. The other is that she loved him, too."

Her mother dropped her gaze to her hands, to her fingers twisted so tightly together. "Her heart was always bigger than anyone else's," she muttered brokenly.

"Please don't punish her for that, Mom. Don't make her choose between you and Marco. She and Grandpa might not have had the kind of marriage you and Dad do, but they made it work anyway. Don't begrudge her this last shot at happiness with the man who's waited a lifetime for her."

CHAPTER EIGHTEEN

THE WEDDING was over.

Dinner was done, and her parents were preparing for an early departure the next morning. The lights were out in the newlyweds' suite. The air was balmy and still and fragrant. Music drifted into the garden where she sat with Oreste.

"You see, Carly?" he murmured, his voice a caress that stole over her with potent appeal. "You worried for nothing. Everyone got along famously, and we are now related by marriage."

At last able to unwind, she slumped lower in her chair and propped her bare feet on a padded footstool. The one flaw in an otherwise perfect day occurred when her grandmother went missing a scant fifteen minutes before the wedding was due to begin.

Carly had deliberately put off helping Anna into her dress and shoes until the last possible moment, then discovered that the bride and her outfit were nowhere to be found. Her carriage—a golf cart festooned with white satin ribbons and flowers—stood empty on the terrace. Wherever she'd gone, she'd done so under her own steam.

Afraid the excitement had been too much for her and she'd become disoriented or collapsed somewhere, Carly had searched the main floor of the house, the terraces and finally, the Moroccan tent in the garden, where the ceremony and reception were to be held.

A white runner led from the entrance to six white upholstered chairs, set in a semicircle before a linen-draped table with an arrangement of cream roses and freesias. A simple filigree frame, twined with ivy and more roses, arched over the middle two chairs.

In one corner, the photographer made final adjustments to his video camera. In the other, the harpist tuned her instrument. Oreste and Marco stood to one side, chatting with the registrar and translator. But of the bride there was no sign.

At the sight of her, Oreste broke into a smile that would, under normal circumstances, have reduced her to a pool of heat. "Carly, you are a vision!"

She doubted it. Slim-fitting purple silk and high heels weren't designed for sprinting along crushed-gravel paths. "I lost my grandmother," she panted. "She's disappeared."

"Not so," Marco said. "She's upstairs in your parents' room. Your mother took her there to help her with her hair."

Flushed, perspiring and distinctly irritated, Carly sagged against the back of the nearest chair. "I wish someone had thought to let me know that!"

But her annoyance died before it could properly take root, eclipsed by a sudden bloom of hope. Her mother and grandmother were doing what women had done for centuries: bonding over the ritual of preparing a bride to meet her groom. A good omen, surely, that for this day, at least, old resentments and misunderstandings would be put aside.

Producing a handkerchief, Oreste dabbed at Carly's nose with his handkerchief. "Be calm, *bellissima*. All is exactly as it should be. You've done your part and done it well. Come now, and take your place beside me. I see the wedding carriage has arrived."

At his signal, the harpist began to play. A moment later, Anna appeared, escorted not just by Taylor, but by Grace, as well. The three of them paused inside the tent, long enough for Grace to give her mother a nosegay of rosebuds and for the photographer to start the camcorder rolling.

Then, with her daughter and son-in-law supporting her on either side, Anna took the final steps of a journey that had begun almost seven decades earlier.

Her mother and grandmother had done much better than effect the temporary truce she'd hoped for, Carly realized. Somehow, all the fractured pieces of their relationship had been put back together again, the inevitable cracks and chips welded by the love they'd always had.

Oreste caught her hand in his. "Your grandmother looks radiant," he whispered in her ear.

She looks tired, Carly thought. For all that they'd tried to conserve Anna's limited strength, bringing her to this day, this moment, had drained her reserves. Grace had done her best, fluffing her mother's hair softly around her face and touching her cheeks with blusher, but there'd been no disguising the livid tint of the skin around her eyes, more telling yet, the chiffon covering her breast fluttered with each shallow breath she took.

Yet Oreste had it right, too. When she saw Marco, Anna lit up inside.

Get her to the chair, Carly prayed, watching her grandmother's halting progress along the white runner.

Please do not let her wedding day turn into her funeral. She's come this far. Please, God, let her make it the rest of the way.

She glanced at Marco. Though he leaned on his cane, he stood as tall as age and health permitted, steadfastly refusing to sit until his bride reached his side. When she was within touching distance, he handed her into her chair as reverently as if she'd been royalty.

The ceremony began, and without warning Carly started to cry. The tears rolled down her face. The photographer focused his lens on her, faithfully recording for posterity her every melodious sniff, but by the time the vows were exchanged and Anna was, at long last, officially Signora Marco Paretti, with his ring on her finger to prove it, there wasn't a dry eye in the place.

They lunched on baby zucchini, medallions of sea bass, *fiochette* and slivers of featherlight wedding cake decorated with pink sugar roses. They toasted the bride and groom with champagne, and when it was time for the newlyweds to return to the house for their afternoon naps, they went in a shower of rose petals.

As she passed by, Anna gave her little bouquet to Carly, "because, precious, throwing it over my shoulder is a risky undertaking at my age. It might end up in the wrong hands."

Carly had smiled and looked away, pretending not to notice Oreste's intent stare.

"Yes," she said to him now. "It *was* a perfect wedding."

"Not quite. There was no first dance between bride and groom."

She almost laughed. "Well, no—for obvious reasons."

"But in Italy," he said, pulling her up from the chair and

into his arms, "in order not to bring bad luck to the couple, it's traditional for the witnesses to make up for that omission."

The music flowed softly around them. The paving stones were sun-warm beneath her bare feet. Almost as warm as his hands against her skin. He'd discarded his jacket and tie hours ago, and rolled his shirtsleeves midway up his forearms. Her purple dress whispered around her ankles.

His gaze locking with hers, he circled the terrace, holding her so close, he stole the breath from her lungs. Well, why not, she wondered dreamily. He'd already stolen her heart.

"Is this really an Italian custom?" she asked.

"It is now," he said.

She felt herself drowning in pleasure, in the magic of the enchanted evening. He was powerfully, unabashedly aroused, and she herself, damp and quivering. Aware they were close to the point of no return, she said, "Before this goes any further, I want to tell you that if we become lovers tonight, as far as I'm concerned, it will be forever."

"Forever is all I ask, *angelo mio*," he said and brought his mouth to hers.

WATCHING GRACE and Anna say goodbye had nearly undone Carly. After too many years of guarded affection and tentative overtures, they lowered their defenses and set themselves free.

Folding her mother in a tender embrace, Grace murmured, "When I heard you and Marco were getting married, I was jealous and hurt because I thought he was taking you away from me. But he loves you very much, and I'd have to be a pretty mean-spirited daughter to resent him for that. Forgive me?"

"Always," Anna said. "And thank you, darling, for blessing me with the dearest wedding present a mother could ask for."

"I love you, Mommy. I always have. And I'm sorry I waited for such a long time to say so."

THE FAREWELLS were made, and Oreste was waiting to drive her parents to the airport.

Red-eyed, now, Grace caught Carly in a last hug. "Promise you'll call. Even if we can't get here before the end, promise you'll call, no matter which of them goes first."

"I promise," she said, breaking down, too, because she knew it was a call she'd be making very soon.

But days became a week, and then a month. Carly the nurse marveled, as she had so often before, at the tenacity of the human spirit to overcome the frailty of the human body. And Carly the woman, who'd believed she was in charge of her future, discovered what her grandmother had learned years ago: that people don't choose when or whom to love. Love chooses them.

Oreste had come into her life without warning and turned it in a direction she hadn't seen coming. Because of him, she now believed that true love was worth whatever price it demanded of those who dared to embrace it.

She witnessed it in the devotion of a dying old man to his dying wife. "I have to go now, my love," she heard her grandmother whisper faintly one evening as August crept to a close. "Until the next time, yes?"

"No," her husband said, somehow mustering the strength to gather her in his arms. "Until forever, *carissima. Ti amo.*"

Carly felt it in the steady gaze of the man who held her

when she cried, and told her he'd cherish her for the rest of time. The unshakable certainty that she'd found her soul mate made it possible to say goodbye to her grandmother, and then, within the month, to Marco. Without Anna at his side, he quietly turned his face to the wall, died in mid-September and was laid to rest beside her.

Remaining with Oreste at the grave site after the other mourners had gone, Carly said, "Their love was their greatest and most enduring legacy."

"And now it's ours to nurture and pass on to our children We owe them so much, *tesoro mio*."

"We owe them everything," she said, accepting without reservation what her grandmother had always known. The power of love was larger than life and greater than death.

It was eternal.

EPILOGUE

IN THE FOUR years since she'd buried her grandmother, Carly had known much happiness. She'd walked down the aisle, a bride on her father's arm, in the same Moroccan tent where Anna and Marco had exchanged their vows. She'd snagged the most wonderful man in the world as her husband and with him had discovered the deep joy that comes from true intimacy, lasting love.

They had an adorable twenty-month-old son, Steven Marco Paretti, who filled their days with sunshine. Yet within the idyllic tapestry of Carly's life remained a slight imperfection, a tiny emptiness that no degree of contentment quite managed to disguise. Until the bright April morning that Oreste placed their newborn daughter in her arms.

The child had her father's dark hair and her brother's flawless skin. But the blue eyes staring up at her mother were filled with wisdom, an old soul's in a brand-new body.

Carly recognized that gaze and a wonderful sense of completeness streamed through her. "Hello, my baby," she crooned. "Hello, my beautiful Anna."

Life had come full circle. The emptiness was filled at last.

* * * * *

Here's a sneak peek at
THE CEO'S CHRISTMAS PROPOSITION,
the first in USA TODAY *bestselling author*
Merline Lovelace's HOLIDAYS ABROAD *trilogy*
coming in November 2008.

American Devon McShay is about to get the Christmas
surprise of a lifetime when she meets her new client,
sexy billionaire Caleb Logan, for the very first time.

Silhouette
Desire

Available November 2008

Her breath whistled out in a sigh of relief when he exited customs. Devon recognized him right away from the newspaper and magazine articles her friend and partner Sabrina had looked up during her frantic prep work.

Caleb John Logan, Jr. Thirty-one. Six-two. With jet-black hair, laser-blue eyes and a linebacker's shoulders under his charcoal-gray cashmere overcoat. His jaw-dropping good looks didn't score him any points with Devon. She'd learned the hard way not to trust handsome heartbreakers like Cal Logan.

But he was a client. An important one. And she was willing to give someone who'd served a hitch in the marines before earning a B.S. from the University of Oregon, an MBA from Stanford and his first million at the ripe old age of twenty-six the benefit of the doubt.

Right up until he spotted the hot-pink pashmina, that is.

Devon knew the flash of color was more visible than the sign she held up with his name on it. So she wasn't surprised when Logan picked her out of the crowd and cut in her direction. She'd just plastered on her best businesswoman smile when he whipped an arm around her waist. The next moment she was sprawled against his cashmere-covered chest.

"Hello, brown eyes."

Swooping down, he covered her mouth with his.

Sheer astonishment kept Devon rooted to the spot for a few seconds while her mind whirled chaotically. Her first thought was that her client had downed a few too many drinks during the long flight. Her second, that he'd mistaken the kind of escort and consulting services her company provided. Her third shoved everything else out of her head.

The man could kiss!

His mouth moved over hers with a skill that ignited sparks at a half dozen flash points throughout her body. Devon hadn't experienced that kind of spontaneous combustion in a while. A *long* while.

The sparks were still popping when she pushed off his chest, only now they fueled a flush of anger.

"Do you always greet women you don't know with a lip-lock, Mr. Logan?"

A smile crinkled the skin at the corners of his eyes. "As a matter of fact, I don't. That was from Don."

"Huh?"

"He said he owed you one from New Year's Eve two years ago and made me promise to deliver it."

She stared up at him in total incomprehension. Logan hooked a brow and attempted to prompt a nonexistent memory.

"He abandoned you at the Waldorf. Five minutes before midnight. To deliver twins."

"I don't have a clue who or what you're…"

Understanding burst like a water balloon.

"Wait a sec. Are you talking about Sabrina's old boyfriend? Your buddy, who's now an ob-gyn doc?"

It was Logan's turn to look startled. He recovered faster than Devon had, though. His smile widened into a rueful grin.

"I take it you're not Sabrina Russo."

"No, Mr. Logan, I am *not*."

* * * * *

Be sure to look for
THE CEO'S CHRISTMAS PROPOSITION
by Merline Lovelace.
Available in November 2008 wherever books are sold,
including most bookstores, supermarkets, drugstores and
discount stores.

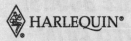

HARLEQUIN®

American ★ Romance®

LAURA MARIE ALTOM
A Daddy for Christmas

THE STATE OF PARENTHOOD

Single mom Jesse Cummings is struggling
to run her Oklahoma ranch and raise her
two little girls after the death of her husband.
Then on Christmas Eve, a miracle strolls onto
her land in the form of tall, handsome bull
rider Gage Moore. He doesn't plan on staying,
but in the season of miracles, anything
can happen....

***Available November
wherever books are sold.***

LOVE, HOME & HAPPINESS

Romantic
SUSPENSE

**Sparked by Danger,
Fueled by Passion.**

Lindsay McKenna
Susan Grant

Mission: Christmas

Celebrate the holidays with a pair
of military heroines and their daring men
in two romantic, adventurous stories
from these bestselling authors.

Featuring:

"The Christmas Wild Bunch"
by *USA TODAY* bestselling author
Lindsay McKenna

and

"Snowbound with a Prince"
by *New York Times* bestselling author
Susan Grant

Available November wherever books are sold.

MARRIED BY CHRISTMAS

Playboy billionaire Elijah Vanaldi has discovered
he is guardian to his small orphaned nephew.
But his reputation makes some people question
his ability to be a father. He knows he must
fight to protect the child, and he'll do anything
it takes. Ainslie Farrell is jobless, homeless and
desperate—and when Elijah offers her a position
in his household she simply can't refuse....

Available in November

HIRED: THE ITALIAN'S
CONVENIENT MISTRESS
by
CAROL MARINELLI
Book #29

www.eHarlequin.com   HPE82375

Inside ROMANCE

Stay up-to-date on all your romance reading news!

The Inside Romance newsletter is a FREE quarterly newsletter highlighting our upcoming series releases and promotions!

Click on the <u>Inside Romance</u> link on the front page of **www.eHarlequin.com** or e-mail us at insideromance@harlequin.ca to sign up to receive your FREE newsletter today!

You can also subscribe by writing us at: HARLEQUIN BOOKS Attention: Customer Service Department P.O. Box 9057, Buffalo, NY 14269-9057

Please allow 4-6 weeks for delivery of the first issue by mail.

IRNBPA208

#1524 SECOND-CHANCE FAMILY • Karina Bliss
Suddenly a Parent

The last thing Jack Galloway wants is to raise a family. But now he's guardian of his late brother's three kids. What does a workaholic businessman know about being a parent? Jack's about to find out when he discovers who his co-guardian is: his ex-wife, Roz!

#1525 CHRISTMAS WITH DADDY • C.J. Carmichael
Three Good Men

Detective Nick Gray has made a career out of playing the field. But unexpected fatherhood has put him to the ultimate test—and he needs help! Lucky for him, Bridget Humphrey steps in as temporary nanny. Can this fun-loving bachelor become a devoted family man? In the season of miracles, anything can happen!

#1526 COWBOY FOR KEEPS • Brenda Mott
Home on the Ranch

Cade misses how Reno used to look up to him, almost like a big brother. But that was when he'd been a deputy sheriff—before he was forced to shoot her stepfather…before he left town, abandoning Reno when she needed a big brother most. Well, now he's back. And Reno needs his help, even if she's too proud to admit it.

#1527 THE HOLIDAY VISITOR • Tara Taylor Quinn

Each Christmas, Craig McKellips stays at Marybeth Lawson's B and B. For those intense days, their relationship grows. But it's jeopardized when he reveals his identity...and his link to her past. Can she forgive the man who could be the love of her life?

#1528 CHRISTMAS IN KEY WEST • Cynthia Thomason
A Little Secret

Abby Vernay's coming home for Christmas—to her eccentric family in Key West. And to the man she's been avoiding for thirteen years. Now chief of police, Reese Burkett is as irresistible as ever. But if they're going to have a future together, she has to come clean about the past. And the secret she's been keeping all this time....

#1529 A CHRISTMAS WEDDING • Tracy Wolff
Everlasting Love

Their daughter's wedding should be among the happiest of days. Instead, Desiree and Jesse Rainwater are barely holding their marriage together. She knows their love is still strong and will do whatever it takes to prove to him they share too much to walk away.